I recommend this excellent novel. Ken Gire not only captures the drama and excitement of small-town high school football, but he also captures the true heart of the game—which has more to do with building character than scoring points.

—Tom Landry

McKinney High, 1946

Also by Ken Gire

The "Moments With the Savior" Series:
Intimate Moments with the Savior
Incredible Moments with the Savior
Instructive Moments with the Savior
Intense Moments with the Savior

When You Can't Come Back
(with Dave and Jan Dravecky)

Miracle of Life
(with Robert and Mary Wells, and Judy Gire)

McKinney High, 1946

by Ken Gire

ZondervanPublishingHouse
Grand Rapids, Michigan

A Division of HarperCollins*Publishers*

McKinney High, 1946
Copyright © 1993 by Ken Gire

Requests for information should be addressed to:
Zondervan Publishing House
Grand Rapids, Michigan 49530

First edition

The hardcover edition of *McKinney High, 1946* was printed in a limited edition of 2000 copies.

Library of Congress Cataloging-in-Publication Data

Gire, Ken
    McKinney High, 1946 : a novel / by Ken Gire.
        p.   cm.
    ISBN 0-310-59040-X. – ISBN 0-310-59041-8 (softcover)
        1. High schools—Texas—Fiction. 2. Football—Texas—Fiction.
    I. Title.
    PS3557.I72M35   1993
    813'.54–dc20
                                                                    93–11430
                                                                        CIP

Published in association with Sealy M. Yates and Associates, Orange, California.

Cover design by Gary Gnidovic and Doug Johnson
Cover Photography by Carlos Vergara Photography

Printed in the United States of America

93 94 95 96 97 98 99 00 / DH / 7 6 5 4 3 2 1

This edition is printed on acid-free paper and meets the American National Standards Institute Z39.48 standard.

To the memory of Coach

McKinney High, 1946

1

A gray '36 Chevrolet rattled down the hot Texas highway, its Kansas license splattered with bugs. Roped to the top of the car were a few spindly pieces of furniture. Crammed into the backseat were boxes of household goods that buttressed an old sewing machine.

Twenty-seven-year-old Pete Williams, dressed in army fatigues, a sweaty T-shirt, and a two-day growth of beard, squinted into the sun as he pulled down the visor to shade the glare on his wire-rimmed glasses. Beth, his wife of eight months, sat next to the window, where air like the blasts from an open furnace riffled through her dark-brown hair.

Pete reached for the knob on the radio, trying to pick up a local station. Static. A scratchy Tommy Dorsey. Static. A faint Andrews Sisters. Static. "Moonlight Cocktail." He stopped there and turned up the volume to drown out the insistent strum of worn pistons.

Beth lifted the hair from her shoulders, letting the wind dry the back of her neck as she called out over the music. "We could at least sign up for it."

"We been over all this before, Beth; I told you, I'm not takin' a handout."

"You don't have to take it. It'd just be nice knowing we had something to fall back on if things don't work out."

"They'll work out."

She leaned over to see the gas gauge. Empty. She looked at Pete, then through his window caught sight of a dead armadillo on the shoulder of the road, its legs extended stiffly into the air. A lanky buzzard stood over it like a shabbily dressed undertaker taking measurements.

"Gauge is broke. Way I figure, we got twenty, twenty-five miles worth of gas."

Beth tried to open the glove compartment, but it wouldn't budge. "Does anything on this car work?" She pried at it for a minute, then Pete reached over and hit the corner with the palm of his hand, popping it open.

"Somethin'll turn up, Beth. Texas is wide open with opportunity. We just gotta keep lookin', that's all."

She rummaged around in what looked more like a rat's nest than a glove compartment and dug out a road map.

"There was a station in Sulphur Springs."

"We'd be backtrackin' then." Pete pointed to a road sign. GREENVILLE—20 MILES. "We can fill up in Greenville."

She leaned over for another look at the gauge. "It's just five miles back."

"We'll make it."

They traveled down the interstate, heat swimming up from its surface. Seeping with tar, the road was bordered with a regiment of creosoted poles, strung together by a tired sag of telephone line. The fields were expansive wastes of black, cloddy dirt. All that remained from an earlier harvest was stubble made stiff by the scorn of an angry August sun. Tufts of Johnson grass, the only green in the county that hadn't yet given up the ghost, grew up defiantly around the gray fence posts.

Beth stared across the interminable flatness, skimming the monotonous line on the horizon, squinting for any syllable of hope that even came close to spelling "opportunity." But she found none.

The monotony was finally broken by a road sign:

GREENVILLE STRAIGHT AHEAD. Pete leaned over to Beth. "You're gonna like Texas." She mopped her forehead with a wadded-up hanky, unconvinced. "Name comes from the Tejas Indians. Means 'friendly.'"

By the time they came into town, Beth was steering the Chevy on the side of the road, and Pete was pushing. Just before she coasted into the Humble station, they passed under a banner that stretched across the street: GREENVILLE— HOME OF THE BLACKEST DIRT AND THE WHIT- EST PEOPLE.

The gas station attendant looked like a shopworn character off the cover of an old *Saturday Evening Post*. He began filling the tank with nineteen-cent-a-gallon gas and popped the hood. He hosed down the radiator and added water once it cooled enough to ease off the cap. Then he nosed around for the dipstick and added two quarts of oil. Finally, after tightening a fan belt, he lowered the hood. He wiped his hands on a limp, oil-smudged rag. "Let's see, with the oil . . . comes to four-thirty-two."

Pete dug into his pocket and minced out the change into the man's outstretched palm. He reached for his billfold and thumbed the corners of the remaining bills, adding up the last remnant of his army pay. Thirty-five dollars. He pulled out four ones and reluctantly surrendered them.

"Yawl come back, ya hear?" the attendant said.

Pete nodded and turned to see Beth through the windshield, asleep, her head cradled on the seat, her face flushed and pinpricked with sweat. He turned to the atten- dant. "Where's the uh, the nearest uh—"

"Unemployment office?" said the man whose eyes took cursory note of the license plate. Pete nodded. "I don't know how they do things up North, but we go by the Good Book down here: 'A man don't work, he don't eat.'"

"But if he don't eat, he can't do much work," Pete said, trying to bridge the awkward moment with a little humor.

But the attendant's leathery face didn't crack a smile, so Pete changed his tone. "Look, I'm wantin' work, not a handout. I'm a veteran. Just tryin' to get a start, that's all."

The man looked at Pete's army-green khakis and extended his lanky arm in a westerly direction. "McKinney. Yonder some twenty miles. Stay on 24 and it'll take ya there."

The town was located forty miles north of Dallas, which, to most people in McKinney, wasn't near north enough. It was a bustling town of ten thousand, at least it bustled as much as a town could in the swelter of a Texas summer. As the county seat of Collin County, McKinney was a hive of weekday activity, abuzz with courthouse business and the shuffle of clerical papers. The city boasted a flour mill, a pecan-cracking plant, a peanut-patty factory, and a couple of cotton gins. The biggest employer in the city was the Texas Textile Mill. The town had two hospitals, Ashburn General and a V.A. hospital north of town. There was one graveyard and two funeral parlors that competed for the bodies of the deceased. Competing for their souls were churches of every major denomination, from Pentecostals to Presbyterians, from the once-saved-always-saved Baptists to the not-so-sure-if-they-are Methodists.

Beth slept the entire way. As the Chevy slowed to survey the town square, she woke up, yawning as they passed the Ritz Theatre. The marquee advertised *Without Reservations,* a movie with John Wayne and Claudette Colbert, billing it as "a cross-country romantic escapade."

"Where are we?"

"McKinney."

Across the street was Gambrel's Drugstore where booths of teenagers sipped cherry Cokes from soda straws and snitched french fries from one another. They eased by the front of Finney's Bakery where a seduction of pies and pastries were displayed in the window. They passed Compton's Grocery with its advertisements of Aunt Betty Bread for ten cents a loaf, roast beef for thirty-nine cents a pound, and butter for sixty-nine cents. They rolled by F. W. Woolworth's with its striped awning that ran the length of the storefront, offering shady respite to a few old-timers whiling away the afternoon on wooden benches.

Pete spotted the sign he was looking for: Texas Unemployment Compensation Commission. He pulled into a parking space and got out to open Beth's door.

"I'll just stay here and read," she said, pulling a book from her purse.

"Shouldn't take long."

In the government office Pete filled out a ream of forms. An hour slowly sweated by before he returned to the car. "Gonna take eight to ten weeks to process the paperwork."

Beth blotted a broken necklace of sweat that the heat had strung under her chin. "Did they have any jobs?"

"Said something about an opening at the high school."

The high school was three stories of rusty red brick, a Works Progress Administration project built during the Depression by stockbrokers, bankers, and brick masons, all working side by side, each feeling lucky to even have a job. The windows were tall rectangles of custodial neglect, a summer's worth of dirt silted on the outside. The white columns flanking the front door were thirsting for paint. But the district was, as they say, "too poor to paint and too proud to whitewash," so the stately columns just stood there, maintaining their Southern dignity as they slowly turned to chalk.

Once in the office, Pete was given a form by the secretary. As he sat in a worn wooden desk to fill it out, he heard voices from behind the door to the superintendent's office. An old, palsied fan oscillated in the corner, but it did nothing to cool the heat coming from the half-inch opening under the door. The voices grew louder, and the sound of someone slapping a table caused Pete to drop his pencil. He looked up at the secretary.

"Emergency meeting of the school board," she explained, and then the voices became more distinct.

"Two years without a win isn't a dry spell, Charlie. It's a drought. I say we plow it under; let it lay fallow a couple o' years."

"I've heard all kinds of dumb in my life, Willard, but that one goes right up on the top shelf."

"We got no boys that can hit, 'ceptin' the Thompson kid, an' he's ineligible. We got no money for uniforms—"

"And we got no coach," added another voice.

"The school can't afford to bring in someone from out of town."

"An' nobody local's gonna touch it with a cane pole."

Pete shifted his weight, fidgeting like a kid sent to the principal's office and suddenly realizing the big trouble that awaited him. A thought flashed through his mind: *If I hurry, I could make Dallas before dark.*

But as he stood to leave, the superintendent's door opened. Four men filed out of the office, grumbling their complaints into their hats as they put them on. Willard Kincaid, treasurer of the school board, bumped into Pete on his way out.

"Excuse me," said Pete, but Kincaid just looked at him and walked away.

After the last of the board members left the office, the secretary snagged the superintendent's attention. "Mr. Stedman, a Mr. Williams is here to see you—"

Ignoring Pete, he handed her a letter. "I need this typed and—"

"He came to inquire about a job."

"—sent out in today's mail."

Miss Carpenter took the letter and smiled. "He played football."

"College football?" Mr. Stedman asked, turning to Pete. "Kansas State Teachers' College."

Stedman's face softened, and he ushered the new prospect into his office. "So, you're from out of town."

Beth, meanwhile, was trying to fight off the distraction of the heat as she read, pulling at her clinging cotton dress to air it out.

An hour later the superintendent emerged from his office, his arm draped paternally around Pete's shoulder. "Well, you have to take into consideration it costs less to live in these parts—a lot less."

When Pete came to the car, Beth was fanning herself with her book. He leaned into her window and smiled. "I got it."

"You what?"

"I got the job—coaching football and teaching four classes of history!"

"Oh, that's great! That's wonderful!" She cupped her hands around his face and kissed him. When their lips parted, hers grew suddenly practical. "How much does it pay?"

Pete walked around to the driver's side and got in. As he started the car, she probed him, "It does pay, doesn't it?"

He looked in the rear-view mirror and began backing up. "Pays regular, first of the month."

"How much?"

"Well, you have to take into consideration it costs less to live in these parts—a lot less."

2

Pete drove to the football field, and all the way there the discussion about salary continued. "They paid you more than that in the service," Beth said as they got out of the car. "In the service I got bombs dropped on me. At least I don't have to worry about that—" The sight of the field put a pause in his voice. "—here."

The field looked like the aftermath of a German blitzkrieg. One goalpost was down; the other leaned precariously to the right. The bleachers were dilapidated. The ground was rutted and covered with patches of brown grass that had surrendered to an army of bull nettles and stickers. From the distant end zone a derelict scoreboard stared back at them.

"Ask for a raise," said Beth.

"He said it would be a rebuilding year," Pete mumbled blankly.

"A big raise."

"He said it would be a challenge; he told me that."

"And tell him if you don't get it, you're moving on to Dallas. Our bags are still in the car, packed. It wouldn't be any trouble to get back on the highway and put all this in our rear-view mirror." Pete was still in a daze as Beth spoke. She came over and stood straight in front of him. "Pete, Texas is full of opportunity. Something will come up. We just gotta keep looking.' Remember? We don't have to take the first thing that comes down the pike."

"I took the job, Beth. I promised the superintendent I'd do my best to turn things around. You don't want me to go back on my word, do you?"

She took a second look at the field, the bleachers, the goalpost, then turned to him. "Yes."

Pete took her hands in his. "We been on the road a long time, Beth. Looked at a lot of places. Applied for a lot of jobs. This is the only one made us an offer." He ran his hands tenderly up her arms and paused as his eyes rested on hers. "Didn't offer much, I grant you that, but it's somethin'; it's a start."

For the remainder of the afternoon they sat in Gambrel's Drugstore, sipping coffee as they combed through the *Daily Courier Gazette* for a place to live. She sipped hers from the cup; he sipped his from the saucer.

The "no deposit required" ad was the one that caught their eye. A three-room "efficiency."

The three rooms, they found when they answered the ad, were attached to the landlady's house. Unlocking the door, Sue, the landlady, led them to a Spartan but well-kept living room. Pete tried to bolster Beth's already sagging enthusiasm for the place. "A phonograph." But it registered as only a small compensation in her eyes.

Sue led them into the bathroom with its claw-foot tub and freestanding sink.

"Does it come with a washing machine?"

"You're lookin' at it," said Sue, pointing to the tub. Beth looked over to Pete.

"Whaddya say we take a look at the kitchen," he said, squeezing himself out of the narrow doorway and into the hall. Sue led them to the small kitchen, which consisted of a sink, a cupboard, and a double hot plate.

"There's no stove," Beth whispered to Pete.

"It'd just heat up the place. Ya don't want that, do ya?" Before Beth could answer, Sue was off to the bedroom, where the bed and a chest of drawers took up the entire room. Beth groped for the right words. "It's, it's uh ..." "Twenty-four dollars a month," said Sue. "In advance." Before Beth could say another word, Pete had his billfold open and was peeling off the rent. "We'll take it."

Shortly after they moved in, while Beth was in the living room reading a magazine and listening to the phonograph, Sue flung open the screen door. She shot a hard look at Beth and went over to lift the needle off the record. "Phonograph's for your personal use; not to entertain the whole neighborhood."

"I'm sorry, I didn't—"

"I turn in early and I'm a light sleeper, so don't go playin' it after dark."

"I'll try to be more—"

"A small town's got its ways. Ya wanna get along in a small town, you abide by its ways. Livin' in a small town's like this here china cabinet." And she shook it lightly. "Ya rattle around a little and everyone hears about it. Ya hear who's a whiskey-drinkin' Baptist, which Methodists are fallin' from grace and why, who's covetin' his neighbor's wife and how often." She opened the door where the cups hung from little hooks, and the saucers and plates and bowls were neatly stacked. She took a cup off the hook.

"Everybody's got a place in a small town. Ya don't wanna go lookin' for a cup and find somebody's put it in the silverware drawer. No, ya go lookin' for a cup and ya wanna find it right where ya left it. People here don't go changin' neighborhoods or churches or try to squeeze in somewheres they ain't meant to be. They find a place where they fit, and they stay put." She hung the cup back on its hook. "Where do Pete and I fit in?"

"Where you be suits you fine," Sue said and turned to leave. "Remember what I said 'bout the phonograph."

The next morning Pete drove to the high school. If he was going to rebuild the football program, he wanted to know how far down he had to dig to lay the foundation. His first stop was the locker room. A mop bucket stood sentry at the door, guarding the slippery entrance. Pete moved the handle of the mop to one side and entered the cavernous room. He picked his way around the puddles of standing water, noticing, as he did, thin shards of paint that curled away from the walls. Above the sink was a mirror, webbed with cracks. A row of bent, rusty nails served as a towel rack outside the shower. Pete stepped inside. It was a greenhouse of mildew with riverbeds of rust running down the walls from the plumbing fixtures. An old washing machine stood plumply in the corner, chugging away and emitting intermittent sparks from its exposed motor.

The air in the locker room was thick with heat and stale with humidity. As Pete blotted his face with a handkerchief, a disembodied voice bounced off the walls.

"Hut one, hut two."

He turned in time to see a tightly wound towel arc through the air and plunk into a clothes hamper in the corner. A white stubby dog, half-boxer, half-bulldog, stood in front of it and jumped to catch the towel, but it was too much of a stretch and he nipped only air.

"Touchdown!" came the voice, followed by the imitation of a crowd cheering. The dog barked his protest. Pete cut his eyes to the left, to the right. The phantom voice returned.

"He's going for two! The crowd's on its feet."

Pete inched his head out the other end of the tiled shower. He saw a dwarf from behind, squatting as if taking a snap from center and whose hands held a wadded-up towel.

"He studies the Highland Park defense. Hut one!" As

the boy dropped back to pass, he suddenly made eye contact with Pete. Startled, he let out a truncated scream—which, in turn, startled Pete, who responded in kind and flinched back behind the shower wall. The dog scrambled over the floor and started barking.

"Quiet, Fibber! Stop it!"

The boy eased his head around the corner, holding the dog by the collar. The dog growled, and the boy slapped him on the snout. "You must be the new coach."

"You're not the quarterback, are you?" Pete asked, a tinge of apprehension in his voice.

"Nope," he said. "Manager." Pete breathed a sigh of relief. "The name's Button. Billy Button. And this here's Fibber."

"Williams. Pete—" He corrected himself and shook Billy's hand. "Coach Williams. I take it Highland Park's the big rival."

"Yep."

While they talked, Pete helped gather the loose towels and put them in the washer. The machine strained like a transmission stuck in first gear. Billy dragged the equipment box beside it and stepped up to drop in his load of towels.

"They any good?"

Billy stepped down and got a broom handle to poke into the exposed viscera of the machine. After a few jabs the gears changed. A spark flew from the machine, and Pete jumped back. "They always win conference; last year won state." Billy opened the equipment box, got out a spool of tape and went about repairing the wire.

"How'd we do against 'em?"

"Really wanna know?"

Pete nodded. Billy went to the equipment cage and got down a canister of film and an old 8 mm projector. "Put some towels over the windows; I'll set up the projector."

Towel by towel the locker room grew dark. When the

last towel was in place, a widening funnel of light cut through the darkness, illuminating airborne particles of dust and throwing a radiant square of light onto the wall. The clackety-clack of poorly aligned sprockets echoed through the locker room as the slender train of celluloid relived last year's game with Highland Park.

Jerky and at times out of focus, the amateur film sent a chaos of images crawling over the wall. Highland Park, looking like a college team by comparison, fielded the kickoff with an impressive return. On the first play from scrimmage the quarterback dropped back to pass in a well-protected pocket. As McKinney rushed, they were solidly blocked. Three of the linemen were knocked down completely, and when they got up, were flattened once again. The ball arced over the defensive secondary, and the Highland Park end, without breaking stride, caught it and skirted down the sidelines into the end zone. The point-after was good, and the shaky camera panned left to find the scoreboard: HOME 7— VISITOR 0.

"Where'd ya get this?"

"Byron Jeffers' dad filmed it. Byron's the one fielding the kickoff."

As soon as Jeffers caught the ball, he was hit by a pack of Highland Park Scotties. The ball squirted into the end zone, and the Scotties fell on it. Once again the camera searched for the scoreboard: HOME 13—VISITOR 0.

The film was a crash course on McKinney football, and Billy stood next to the wall, pointing out the Lions' offensive plays and defensive strategy, neither of which worked that night. He commented on each of the players, noting their strengths and weaknesses and untapped potential. Finally the tail end of film threaded through the projector to frame McKinney's fate: HOME 87—VISITOR 7. As if suddenly swept clean of the past, the wall turned brilliantly white again.

"McKinney bites the dust again," said Billy as he began pulling towels off the windows.

"Bite it? I'd say we made a meal of it—a sit-down, Sunday meal." Pete helped pull down the towels. "But that was last year; boys can grow up a lot in a year."

"Lot of 'em thinkin' 'bout not goin' out."

"Well," said Pete, smiling, "we'll just have to change their minds, won't we?"

Billy smiled back. "I reckon so."

Pete took Billy with him to meet those who were going out for the team and to stir up interest for those who weren't. Their first stop was the Thompson place, a cotton farm about two-and-a-half miles outside of town. It was the home of Gill Thompson, the senior lineman who was the only bright spot on last year's squad.

"He was the best lineman in the district last year. Problem was, the rest of our linemen were the worst." Billy pointed out the window. "Left here. Took a lot of wind out of everyone's sails when we found out he was ineligible."

Pete hit his brakes, inciting a riot of dust around the car. "If he's ineligible, why are we driving out to see him?"

Billy shrugged his shoulders, suddenly self-conscious. "I dunno. I just thought, well, maybe you could do somethin' to help him, that's all."

"What did he fail?"

"English. Ol' lady—Miss Caulfield's class." Pete put the car in gear and continued down the dirt road.

"What's she like?"

"Tough as a cob if you get on her bad side."

"Any advice?"

"Stay off her bad side," he said with a smile.

Tall stalks of Johnson grass bordered both sides of the post oak fence leading to the Thompson place. The roofline of the barn sagged like a put-out-to-pasture horse, too sway-backed to saddle. Its whitewash had all weathered off, and its door hung unsteadily on one hinge. Peeking out of the door, looking considerably less than contented, was a scraggly milk cow.

The farm, it seemed, had produced a bumper crop of kids—here a kid, there a kid, everywhere they looked, a kid—eight that they could count, and they suspected they hadn't counted them all. They were shy and barefoot and all whispers of curiosity as the car drove up to the house. A few chickens protested the intrusion with a ruffled display of feathers. The others made way and went about their business, pecking around the yard.

Pete and Billy got out of the car, walked up the steps and across the loosely planked porch where a sow was shading herself under the porch, her litter snuffling over the soft, pink flesh as the runt jockeyed in frantic search of an opening.

They looked through the tattered screen door to see a starkly furnitured living room, its floor strewn with pillows and blankets and thinly stuffed pallets. On the table stood an empty bottle of whiskey. Pete knocked, and a six-year-old pair of bare feet came padding to the door.

The boy was wearing hand-me-down overalls that, from the looks of them, had been handed down a few times too often. They were frayed at the ends, grinning at the knees, and clinging to only a dim memory of blue.

"Hello."

"Howdy."

"Your parents home?"

"Mamma's at the Jocko Lot, sellin' okra."

"And your daddy?"

"Asleep. Want I should git 'im fer ya?" The boy's eyes fell on Billy's short legs.

"No. Is your brother around?"

"Which 'un? I got a passel."

"Gill."

The boy pointed. "Out yonder a ways, hoein'."

They drove where the young boy had pointed, but the only person they saw hoeing was a barefoot, teenage girl in a washed-out cotton dress and sunbonnet. Pete stopped the car and got out. He turned and asked, "You comin'?"

Billy looked at the girl and then at Pete. "I'll just wait."

Pete plodded through the furrows of rich earth as cicadas in a nearby windbreak complained about the heat. He nodded his greeting to the shy-looking girl. "Gill anywhere around?"

"Down by that pecan tree over there, last time I saw."

The branches of the tree formed a sprawling circle of shade where Gill lay on his back, asleep. He was two-hundred-and-thirty pounds of prime Texas beef, spread out over six feet, four inches. A hat covered the boy's bush of red hair and shaded the freckled ruddiness of his face. The smoldering butt of a cigarette dangled loosely from his lips.

Pete cleared his throat. "You Gill Thompson?" The boy shot to his feet, sweeping the cigarette behind his back. As he did, he singed himself and grimaced. "I'm Pete Williams, the new football coach." He extended his hand. Clumsily, Gill switched the cigarette into his left hand, burning himself again as he did.

"Glad to know ya," he said, shaking hands as smoke ascended in wispy apparitions behind him.

"Heard a lot of good things about you, Son."

The remark pleased Gill, who struggled to find the appropriate reply. "Well, I, eh—"

"Lotta good things."

"Thank you, sir. I, I'd like to go out, but, eh—"

"I know about your grades. I'm gonna talk to Miss Caulfield and see what we can do." The smoke continued weaving in the air.

"Won't much matter. M'daddy's gonna need me to help around here."

"Do you want to play?"

"If I could, yessir."

"I'll talk to your daddy too."

"Much obliged . . . Coach." And from behind his back he flicked the cigarette to the ground.

Pete and Billy drove next to the home of Al "Freight Train" Jones. At five-feet-seven, one-hundred-sixty pounds, the stocky boy had a low center of gravity and was just beginning to come into his own. Pete talked with Al and his dad at the family's feed store, just off the town square.

"It's not a land-office business, mind you, but it's steady. Animals got to eat purty much every day," said Mr. Jones with a glint in his eye.

"So tell me," Pete said to the man's son who had just finished stacking ten fifty-pound bags of oats in front of the store, "how'd they come to nickname you 'Freight Train?'"

"I dunno," he said, taking out a bandanna and wiping his brow, "just somethin' kinda tagged along with me as I was growin' up."

"Used to race the train as it blowed by town," said his dad. "Still do, don't ya, Son?"

"Ever' now and then."

"If we're gonna turn things around this year, we'll be needin' somebody with a head o' steam in the backfield. Can we count on ya?"

"When nobody stepped in to fill Coach's shoes, I ended up decidin' to just cart feed after school." Al looked at his dad.

"Well, looks like them shoes done been filled," he said. "And looks like I won't be needin' an extra hand till, let's see, when does the season end—"

"November," said Pete.

"—till sometime in November anyway."

Al wiped his hand with the bandanna and extended it to Pete. "When do we start?"

"Two-a-days start Monday," Pete said to Byron Jeffers, on whose front porch he and Billy sat. A live-oak tree spread over the front lawn and cast its shade on the porch, bringing with it a gentle breeze. "We're gonna be spendin' nights in the gym, up at seven-thirty, on the field by nine, break for lunch, a little skull practice, then back on the field from four to six."

"Ain't gonna be no flies on those boys," said Byron's dad, who worked as a surveyor for the county.

"Not for two weeks anyway," said Pete.

"More cookies?" asked Byron's mother, holding out the tray.

"Thanks," said Billy. "Don't mind if I do."

"Thank you, Mrs. Jeffers."

"Now don't go 'mister' and 'missin'' us, Coach Williams. It's Lynell and Bob, ya hear?"

Billy took a swallow of milk to wash down the cookie. "So whaddya say, Byron?"

"Count me in."

Pete and Billy visited several other boys that day. Their last stop was the home of John Henry "Cheetah" Brown. As they passed the time on his front porch, waiting for him to come home, Cheetah was finishing up the last street on his paper route. He rolled a newspaper, threw it end over end, and it landed in the gutter of a roof.

"High and outside. Ball one," said Cheetah as he swaggered down a dirt street. Normally he would have thrown another paper to replace it, but this was the Woodson house, a house he always had trouble collecting from. "Come back payday," ol' lady Woodson would say. Or "I thought I paid you last week." Other times she wouldn't answer the door at all. No doubt, she would deduct the cost of the errant paper from her monthly bill, but he figured it a small price to pay for the thought of her teetering on some rickety step-ladder to retrieve it.

Cheetah dug into the canvas bag slung around his

shoulder for another paper to fold. It was a long route that left the tongues of his tennis shoes lolling for relief. Tired socks relaxed around his ankles. He was lean and awkward looking, his arms hanging a little too long from his shoulders, his ears cupping out a little too much from his head. His T-shirt was smudged with newsprint, and a sheaf of summer hair hung in his eyes. When he swept it to one side, he spotted a stray cat scavengering through a disgorged garbage can. A smile crept across his face. He rolled the paper tightly and tied a string around it. He checked the bases to the left of him, then to the right, before he delivered his pitch. A fastball. It packed a wallop that sent the stray off in a tirade.

"Steeeeeeeeerike!"

The cat sprinted down the furrows of frame houses that comprised the lower back forty of McKinney—the Mill District. The Mill District was the neighborhood that grew up around the textile mill, made up of hedgerows of houses that had gone to seed. White trash collected there like windblown litter on a chain-link fence. "Lintheads," they called them, from the airborne particles of cotton that got caught in their hair as they worked in the mill.

At the next house a girl was sweeping the porch. "Looking mighty swell today, Connie Sue." She paused to glance up at Cheetah, then went back to her work. "Had a dream about you last night." Still she refused him the dignity of a reply. "Dreamt you were upset and wouldn't gimme the time of day." She continued sweeping. "Wanna know why?" She turned her back and disciplined the porch with her angry broom. "We were at the Rockpit, an' you were wantin' a bounce in the backseat, pressurin' me real bad. But I said I wasn't that kind of boy an' that I was savin' myself. That's when you got upset." She whipped around and glared at him. When she did, Cheetah hurled his paper. She tried to slap it down with her broom, but it got past her and hit the clapboard siding.

"Swing and a miss. Strike two," he said as he whistled his way down the ragged street to the next house. He rolled another paper, this one for the Billingsworths. Mrs. Billingsworth was a cook at the school cafeteria, and her husband, a janitor at the mill. They had one son, Russel. He had dropped out his junior year to train for the Golden Gloves, but the trainer at the gym insisted he cut his ducktail off, and Russel thought that too high a price to pay to be a contender, so he quit. Cheetah had always been one of his favorite punching bags, mainly because he was the only one with spunk enough to fight back, which made it seem more like a legitimate sport than simple bullying.

As the Billingsworths' front porch came into range, Cheetah envisioned their welcome mat as home plate. But the pitch got away from him and went shattering through the window.

"Inside. Ball two," he said under his breath as he broke into a trot.

The screen door exploded and out shot Russel. "I'm gonna whop you, Cheetah Brown!"

Cheetah tore out running, his bag thumping against his thigh. "Gonna havta catch me first, linthead!" he yelled over his shoulder. Cheetah threw out a few rolled-up papers to impede the pursuit, but the bigger boy was gaining fast.

When Russel caught up with him, he rode Cheetah to the ground like a rodeo cowboy bulldogging a steer. There was a furious scuffle, and Russel ended up on top, pummeling Cheetah's face.

"I kin take it out o' yer wallet or I kin take it out o' yer hide—either one'd suit me fine." Cheetah just glowered at him. Russel hit him again. "Want me to take the rest out o' yer wallet?"

Blood leaked from Cheetah's nose and out the corner of his mouth. He hesitated, then spit in Russel's face.

"Sorry white trash." He hit Cheetah again, and again.

"Okay, okay."

Cheetah lay there, his bloody nostrils flared in breathy defiance. The boy drew back his fist.

"Want me to get it for ya?"

"Don't bother."

Russel got up and dusted himself off as Cheetah painfully reached for his billfold. When he opened it, Russel wrenched it away from him and lightened it by three dollars. From the Billingsworths' porch came the call of an older man. "That's enough, Russel! Git on home!" The screen door slapped shut, and the man went back inside. Russel threw the empty billfold to the ground.

Cheetah picked it up and then his paper bag. "Run on home to Daddy," he said in one last recalcitrant breath.

Russel looked over his shoulder and smirked, "Least I got one to run home to."

The words thrust themselves mercilessly into an open wound in Cheetah's heart. Cheetah gritted his teeth and swung his paper bag against Russel's back, knocking the boy off his feet. Russel regained his balance and charged, but an uppercut stood him upright, a left to the stomach doubled him over, and a right hook sent him reeling backward into the dirt.

Cheetah stood over him. "Take it back."

The boy was dizzy but not dizzy enough to blur the clenched fists that jutted menacingly from Cheetah's side. "I take it back."

Cheetah stepped over him, picked up his paper bag and the three loose bills that lay in the dirt, and walked away.

Pete and Billy were on Cheetah's front porch, talking with a bunch of the old-age pensioners that Mrs. Brown roomed and boarded at her house. Cheetah's Uncle Clyde leaned against the porch railing, quickly forming his opinion of the young coach. Uncle Clyde was to opinions what Sears and Roebuck was to catalog sales. You name it, and he not only had it, he had it by the dozen. Of course, they're wasn't a big demand for dozens of Clyde's opinions, which may account for why he gave them away so freely. "So, you never coached before," he said as he tapped the tobacco out of his pipe.

"No."

Another man in a rocking chair spoke up. "Bud Smith—now there was a coach." And all the men in their rocking chairs nodded.

"Yep."

"Don't make 'em like that anymore, nosiree-bob," another of the men chimed in.

"He flat knew how to coach."

"'Course he had experience goin' for him."

"That's what won 'em the championship—experience."

"Amen to that," and the man punctuated his sentence with a spit of tobacco.

"And what year was that championship?" Pete asked.

"1909."

"Well, this is 1946. And Bud Smith isn't here anymore. Nobody's here anymore except me. And I may be green, but at least I'm here. And I'm gonna stay here till I turn things around."

A long silence settled on the porch. Billy looked up at Pete, but the sound of a striking match distracted him. Uncle Clyde lit his pipe, sucked in a few short drags, and exhaled a question into the plume of smoke. "And how ya aim to do that?"

Pete looked him straight in the eye. "One boy at a time."

The screen door opened as Mrs. Brown brought out a tray of lemonade. "I'm much obliged yawl came by to talk to my boy, Coach Williams."

"Harness the fight in John Henry," said Uncle Clyde, taking the pipe out of his mouth and pointing it at Pete, "then ya can lay claim to callin' yourself a coach."

"He could make a good ballplayer in time, if he grows some," said Billy. "Kinda uncoordinated, but he's a scrapper."

The sound of the gate swinging open turned their attention to Cheetah, who slowed his steps the closer he got to the porch. His eyes locked momentarily on Pete's, then on Billy's, and finally on his mother.

"Your ears must've been burnin', John Henry," Mrs. Brown said. "We was just talkin' about—"

But her words fell short as she saw his battered face. Her eyes grew heavy, and she sighed. "Worsh up, Son, we got company."

3

Inspired by the new coach, Billy was up early Saturday morning and with the other manager, Hoot Maxwell, started getting the locker room in shape for two-a-days. Billy used a hoe to scrape the peeling walls. Hoot came behind him with a bucket of off-white paint, slathering them down with a sloppy, horsehair brush. Fibber lay atop a heap of towels near the washing machine, blinking an occasional eye in tired approval of their work.

Tomorrow they would scrub down the showers, scour the toilets, and replace the broken mirror above the sink, but today they would be satisfied if they just finished painting. It was dark by the time they finally did. They were bone tired and speckled with paint, but it was Saturday night, and that thought revived them because it meant an evening with the gang at Gambrel's Drugstore.

Saturday night, if you weren't at the Ritz watching this week's movie or at the Rockpit necking, most likely you were at Gambrel's. You went there to feed pocket change to the jukebox and squeeze into crowded booths of girls or into the booths of the boys who tried to impress them.

Billy had just clinked a nickel into the Wurlitzer. Next to it, Willie D. Tidwell stretched out in a booth, a pack of Chesterfields in the sleeve of his T-shirt. He nodded to Billy as he stubbed out the butt of a cigarette and wrapped his hands around the grease-spattered buns of one of Pop Gambrel's cheeseburgers. Billy nodded back, then looked over to the booth where Mary Ellen, Susie, and Kathy sat. He acknowledged them with a smile as the song "Candy" began playing. It was his favorite, and whenever he heard it he thought of Kathy. She was wearing bobby socks with saddle oxfords and a pale yellow skirt with a thin white sweater that gently caressed her silken skin. Her blonde hair gathered softly on her shoulders. To Billy, she was like a movie star who had just stepped off a picture-show screen. He winked at her as he walked back to his booth.

"Ya know, the jukebox does play other songs," said Byron. "What is that, three times tonight already?"

"My nickel," said Billy.

"But it's *our* ears," said Hoot. "And if they hear that song one more time, we're gonna have to get 'em checked for cavities."

Their bantering was interrupted when Pop came with the girls' order: a tray full of hamburgers, french fries, and cherry Cokes. Thinking a few fries might fall their way if they acted quickly, the boys crowded into the girls' booth.

"Ready for two-a-days?" Susie asked.

"Fixin' to get ready," answered Byron. "We start Monday mornin'." The boys looked at each other and groaned.

"How's the new coach?" asked Kathy.

"Billy knows him best," said Byron.

"He's swell. I think he's gonna work out okay."

"I heard he's never coached before," said Connie Sue.

"That don't mean nuthin'," Billy said, defensively. "And don't let anyone tell ya it does. Hide and watch; he's gonna turn things around."

Heads turned when Cheetah walked by the window, mimicking a chimpanzee and pressing his face against the paned glass. The girls threw a couple of french fries at him, and Cheetah jumped up and down, slumping his shoulders and scratching at his ribs. He shuffled through the door, swinging his long arms and making chimp noises. He played the moment for all it was worth, snitching french fries from every table he passed.

"Hiya, gang," he said, squeezing into their booth. "Hello, Connie Sue." But she turned her head. "Can't stay mad at me forever."

She turned and shot him a look. "Wanna bet?"

The waitress came while Kathy was trying to change the subject. "So, Cheetah, you goin' out for football?"

"Do the French fry? Does a root beer float?"

"What'll it be?" asked the waitress.

"French fries and a root beer float," he said with a wink. To the others he announced confidently: "The Cheetah will be there." He looked over at Willie D. and raised his voice. "Me and Willie D. both'll be there. Right, Willie D.?" Willie D. had just lit up again. He took a long drag, exhaled a billow of smoke, and nodded. While everyone was looking over at Willie D., Cheetah grabbed the hamburger off Kathy's plate.

"Cheetah!" she said, scolding him.

"Put it back," said Billy.

Cheetah took a bite. Billy yanked the burger out of his hands and put it back on Kathy's plate.

"Hey, call off your dog, Jeffers," he said. "Down, boy, down."

"I just wanted a bite," Cheetah told her.

"You can keep your germs to yourself, thank you."

"Not like we never swapped spit before," he said as he chewed. "Remember?" The remark embarrassed her.

"Leave her alone," bristled Billy.

"Come on, Brown, lay off," said Byron.

"Anytime you think you're big enough to make me lay off, Jeffers, you know where to find me."

"Yeah, the Mill District."

"Wanna make somethin' of it?"

"It isn't worth makin' somethin' of."

Cheetah lunged across the table, sending dishes and glasses crashing to the floor. Hoot and Billy tried to separate the two, but it took Pop Gambrel pulling Cheetah out of the booth to stop the fight. He took him by the arm and pushed him out the door. "I told you if I ever caught you fightin' in here again, you'd be out for good! Now git out!"

Bright and early Monday morning the locker room was alive with activity, boys trying on their practice uniforms for the first time since last year. They threaded their arms into shoulder pads and helped each other pull shrunken jerseys over them. They pulled and squeezed and tugged, but few seemed to fit. Either the jerseys were too tight or the shoulder pads too bulky.

Soon a line formed in front of the equipment cage. Hoot was in the cage, digging around in a heap of mismatched uniforms, while Billy stood in front on an equipment box, coordinating the effort. The first boy in line had an old leather helmet that was sitting halfway on his head, askew.

"Got any other headgear?"

Billy called out: "Need a helmet, extra large." Hoot rummaged around and tossed one to Billy, who exchanged it with the boy. "Try this 'un."

A new kid who hadn't gone out for football before was trying to figure out where to put two of the pads. He had positioned them on his ribs when Byron gently took them from the boy's hands and fitted them into the inner pockets of his pants. The boy looked up sheepishly. "Thanks."

"First time I tried 'em on I couldn't figure 'em out either."

Billy looked at his watch, picked up his wooden paddle, and slapped it hard against the equipment box. "Ten till, everybody! Clear the locker room! Don't want to be late for the first workout." He slapped the paddle again, and this time Fibber barked, as if to echo the command. "Come on, boys. Shake a leg. Don't want the new coach to think we're a bunch of lollygaggers. Let's go!" Billy roved through the locker room, whacking the benches with his paddle. Fibber followed right behind him, barking orders like a drill sergeant.

The boys walked seven blocks to the practice field. They walked in their street shoes, carrying their cleats so as not to wear them out on the asphalt. Willie D. took a final pull on the nub of a cigarette and let it drop inconspicuously from his side.

As the boys trickled onto the field, they threw a couple of footballs around to limber up. But when Pete drove up with Billy, Hoot, and Fibber, they put the balls down and drew together in curious knots of threes and fours.

Pete blew his whistle. "Okay, boys, let's line up for cal."

The boys fell into a ragged formation for calisthenics. Cheetah was the last to arrive, straggling onto the field and taking his place in the back row. He shed his street shoes and strained to put on his cleats while trying to keep time with the sit-ups.

Pete ran the team through a regimen of warm-up exercises: sit-ups, push-ups, leg lifts, jumping jacks, rocking horses, squat thrusts. Before long the boys were straining with beet-red faces during their sit-ups, sagging in the back as they did their out-of-sync push-ups, and dropping their legs on the leg lifts whenever Pete walked past them.

"Okay, boys, gimme four quick laps." They groaned as they pushed themselves up from the ground. They turned for the outer edge of the field, which put Cheetah in front of the pack, but his lead was short-lived. Last year's halfback, Al Jones, caught up with him. For a moment they ran neck-and-neck.

"It's too early in the mornin' to go breakin' any school

records, Freight Train—let's just start slow and taper off after the first lap, whaddya say?"

But the halfback put it in gear and left Cheetah in his dust. As they trickled onto the field after their laps, Pete blew his whistle. "Okay, boys, huddle up." They circled around him, still panting and holding their sides. He counted them— twenty-four in all—enough for two teams, but just barely. "We're gonna concentrate on offense this season, puttin' points on the scoreboard. I want you dividin' up into two teams, offense and defense. Gimme some linemen." The request resulted in two lines that paired off opposite of each other. "Got a center?" One of the boys raised his hand, and Pete tossed him the ball. "Where's my quarterback? Byron." The boy raised his hand. Once the players were in position, Pete walked them through some plays. He took the snap from center, setting the backfield in motion, and handed off to the fullback.

"Let's go full speed now." Byron stepped up to the center, but the exchange was fumbled. They ran the play again, but this time he turned the wrong way and was run over by the halfback.

"Why don't we work awhile on our passing game," said Pete, changing gears in an attempt to keep the mood of the workout upbeat. "Where are my ends?" Several of the boys raised their hands. Pete pointed to Cheetah. "Go down about thirty yards and run a post pattern."

"Post pattern?"

"Angle-in toward the goalpost."

Cheetah ran full throttle downfield, his long, loping stride a little awkward looking from behind. As he cut toward the goalpost, he stumbled slightly, regaining his balance just in time to meet the ball. He extended his hands to catch the spiraling bullet, but the ball zipped through them and ricocheted off his shoulder pads.

"Next." Another end lined up, ready to go. Pete handed the football to Byron. "Give it a try."

Byron stepped up to the center and took the snap. The end sprinted downfield, tracing the same pattern, and Byron launched the ball into the air. It was a perfect spiral but overshot the receiver by fifteen yards. The effort impressed Pete. "Good arm, Byron. Need to work a little on control."

When practice ended, Pete had everybody line up in rows for windsprints. A row of linemen. A row of ends. A row of backs. Pete blew his whistle, and a row was off and running. He blew it again, and the next row sprinted downfield. By the time he was finished, all of them were bent over, sucking air, and a few were off to the side, puking up the biscuits and gravy they now wished they hadn't eaten for breakfast.

After the workout Pete went to the high school to see if Miss Caulfield was in. The click of his soles on the linoleum echoed down the empty corridor. A janitor was sweeping the hall with a push broom, causing dust to swarm in the shunts of sun that angled in through the tall windows.

"Mornin', Coach." They had never met, but it was a small town; news of the new coach had traveled fast.

"G'morning."

"How'd the boys look today?"

"Lot of hard work ahead of 'em."

"Ain't never heard o' no one dyin' o' hard work."

"No." He smiled. "I haven't either." Of course, he had heard of coaches getting run out of town, and he suspected that in Texas they might do worse than that, depending on how bad the season went. Suddenly a question popped into his mind.

"Whatever happened to the last coach?"

"Up and quit two weeks ago. Said somethin' 'bout it bein' time to move on; left for Houston, I think, but never told nobody why."

Pete could think of a few reasons: the dilapidated facilities, the fact that the team hadn't won a game in over two years, the thirteen hundred a year he would have to stretch over the next twelve months, not to mention the heat.

"Could you direct me to Miss Caulfield's room?"

"Sure. Upstairs, let's see, be on your right, three doors down."

When he came to Miss Caulfield's room, he found her tacking up a poster of Shakespeare on the bulletin board. She was a sturdily built woman. *German extraction,* he thought, *maybe Dutch.* Her dress was plain and sensible and buttoned up the neck in a stalwart display of public school decorum. Her hair was pulled back severely and wound tightly in a bun. Her reading glasses rested low on the bridge of her nose.

Pete rapped lightly on the open door. She turned and answered the knock with a wooden-sounding, "May I help you?"

"Yes, ma'am," he said as he walked in. "I'm Pete Williams, the new football coach." He extended his hand and smiled broadly.

"Elaine Caulfield—" She paused a beat, offering her hand and the slightest of smiles. "—the old English teacher. What can I do for you?"

"It's not what you can do for me; it's what you can do for Gill Thompson."

"And what is that?"

"Well," he started to say as he sat on the corner of her desk. She knitted her eyebrows and cleared her throat, pressing her lips into thin lines of disapproval. The tacit scolding brought him to his feet and jostled his confidence just enough to throw his prepared speech off balance. "Gill, he's a senior, an ineligible senior, and eh—"

"Ineligible for what? An education?"

"For football. The grade he got last spring is what's

keepin' him from playin'. I was wondering if you'd reconsider."

"You mean change his grade?"

"Yes, ma'am."

She moved toward him and took off her glasses. "What makes you think that just because a boy can run faster or throw farther or hit harder, he doesn't have to play by the same rules everybody else does?"

"I wasn't sayin' that, Miss Cau—"

"What *were* you saying?"

"I was sayin', cut the boy a little slack."

"He can take the course over again in the spring when it's offered. Like everybody else."

"That'll be too late. He'll miss his senior season."

"You mean he'll miss winning you a few football games."

"If he has a good year, he has a chance at an athletic scholarship. Can you think of any other way a kid like him is gonna get a chance at a college education? His grades gonna get him in? His parents gonna pay his way?"

"He had the same opportunity the other pupils in my class had. If I changed his grade, it wouldn't be fair to them."

"None of them have to share supper with twelve brothers and sisters. Or sleep on pallets on the living room floor. None of them have an alcoholic for a father." He paused, running out of patience with her cold indifference. "It's just a little mark in a grade book."

After thirty years of teaching, Miss Caulfield wasn't about to be sat in some school desk and lectured to. "That *little mark* means something, Mr. Williams, something to me, anyway. And I would like to think it means something to each of my students—"

"Well what it means to one of your students is that he'll never get off that rundown farm. Football is his ticket out of there, Miss Caulfield; his only ticket." He paused, then implored her. "Please, I'm just asking you to—"

"You're asking me to go against my principles."

"No. I'm asking you to rise above them." His tone softened. "Listen, Miss—"

"No, Mr. Williams, you listen to me. I'm not changing his grade—his, or any other athlete's."

4

Pete left, but all the way down the stairs he continued the conversation, talking to himself and punctuating his arguments with sweeping gestures of his hands. At the bottom of the stairs he stopped to vent his frustration on a locker, slapping it with an outstretched palm. It echoed down the hallway, a clanging hollowness that seemed to beckon him . . . beckon him . . . beckon him. . . .

He followed the sound and looked up, seeing in the distance a row of windows spilling sunlight onto the floor. He walked slowly toward it until he stood surrounded by the grainy light. He turned and saw a trophy case where the sun gilded the memories of another era. He stepped closer and peered through the glass that enshrined four faded decades of athletic achievement. His eye caught the trophy for the 1909 district championship. It was the biggest in the case. Behind it was framed the legendary team. *Just kids,* he thought, scrawny little kids no bigger than the ones he had drilled that very morning.

"Fourth one down." The voice of the janitor startled him. "Sorry, didn't mean to spook ya."

"No, that's okay."

"Fourth one down." The janitor pointed to the list of names engraved on the trophy.

Pete squinted to read the name: Ted Murphy.

"That's me," he said. "We were the only unbeaten, untied, unscored-upon team in the history of McKinney High."

"Must've been a great bunch of athletes."

"Good . . . but not great."

"Then how'd you have such a great year?"

"We were a team."

Pete studied the old photograph to see if he could find the man's picture. His eyes traveled slowly across two rows of nameless football players and almost passed over him. But there he was, standing in the back row, a leaner, younger Ted Murphy.

When those eyes looked up, Murphy was halfway down the hall, pushing his mop bucket. "Wait," Pete called out, the words bouncing off the walls. "How'd you become a team?"

The man called back. "Coach. He did it. He made us a team."

The words echoed in Pete's ears. He stared again at the old photograph, this time focusing on the coach. He stared hard, as if to pry from him the secret of his success. *He was a serious man,* Pete thought, *a man who knew what he was doing.* Then his thoughts turned inward: *What am I doing in Texas? And what I am doing coaching football?* He looked up, hoping to ask Murphy another question. But he had turned into one of the classrooms.

"Hey, Murphy, wait up," called Pete as he jogged down the hall after him.

As Pete was setting up a blackboard in the gym, the boys were in the cafeteria eating lunch. The cafeteria was a combination of public school plainness and postwar austerity: rows of wooden tables, their surfaces worn smooth by the lunchtime parade of elbows; a well-postured accompaniment of chairs; a corner trash can, stodgy and gray; a portrait of George Washington, looking as if it had billowed out from a cloud; a dutiful clock standing watch over the entrance, its quiet gears keeping everyone punctual.

The "cafeteria ladies," as they were called, wore hair nets woven as delicately as spider webs. The girths of these pear-bodied women had been cinched tight by the strings of white aprons, the fronts of which bore smeared testimony to the day's toil. The women had been conscripted for the duration of two-a-days to feed the team, which was now filing through the line.

"Wonder what's on the menu," said Freight Train.

"Prob'ly some road kill they shoveled off the highway," said Cheetah.

As they shuffled their way through the serving line, four ladies doled out the meal. One dolloped mounds of mashed potatoes onto the outstretched plates. Another ladled out ponds of white cream gravy. Another spooned generous helpings of canned corn. The last lady in the serving line was Mrs. Billingsworth, who brooded, almost maternally, over the fried chicken.

"How was practice this mornin', Albert?" she asked.

"Good workout," he said as she put two plump pieces of chicken on his plate. "Worked up quite an appetite." He extended his plate to her again. She smiled, stretched her tongs over to grab another piece, and placed it on his plate. "Thank you, Mrs. Billingsworth."

"You're most welcome."

Cheetah was next in line and handed her his plate. "Afternoon, Mrs. B."

Her smile retreated, as did the cheery inflection in her voice. "John Henry." She gave him a wing and handed the plate back.

Cheetah looked at Freight Train's plate and then at his. "Still sore about the broken window, aren't ya?" She looked at him sternly, refusing to serve a reply. "Well, if it makes you feel better, I gave up the paper route—for football." He handed the plate back to her, and reluctantly she gave him another piece. He looked down at the skinny drumstick, disappointed. "I've been meanin' to drop by some Saturday and work off the damage." He handed the plate back to her, and she conceded in giving him a breast portion.

"How about *this* Saturday?"

"Let's just say, *some* Saturday." Before his smile had a chance to broaden, she snatched away the chicken breast with her tongs.

Cheetah momentarily mourned the loss but managed to eat his way out of his grief. As he sat mopping up his cream gravy with a slice of white bread, Billy came by and rapped on the table. "Skull in the gym at quarter till. Bring your notebooks." Cheetah looked at the wall clock—12:42—and stuffed the last soppy morsel into his mouth.

Skull practice was the classroom part of football where Pete diagrammed plays on the blackboard, reviewed rules of the game, and answered any of the boys' questions. In the gym the boys roosted in the bleachers. Billy perched on the bottom bench to the right of the blackboard while Fibber rested by his feet. As Pete diagrammed the first play, the board soon became a jumble of O's and X's, with arrows veering off in different directions to indicate the blocking assignments. The boys scribbled the diagrams into their notebooks at a feverish rate. When he finished the last of the plays, Pete erased the board and wiped the chalk dust from his hands.

"Wanna change gears a minute and talk about what's expected of you, on and off the field." He turned to the board and started a list: "They'll be *no cussing* on the field." He turned again to the board. "And they'll be *no smoking*," he wrote in bold letters. Several of the boys craned their necks at Willie D. on the uppermost bleacher. "It's bad for ya and'll affect your wind," Pete said. He turned to write again. *Yes, sir.* "When I talk to you, I don't want to hear 'Yeah' or 'Yep' or 'Uh huh'; I wanna hear 'Yes, sir.'"

"Private Brown reporting for duty, sir," muttered Cheetah under his breath with a furtive salute, which touched off a suppressed circle of laughter.

"What was that, John Henry?"

"Nuthin', Coach. Just a touch o' indigestion from lunch."

No cutting up in class. "If I get wind of any of you disruptin' class or makin' light of a teacher, I'll run your legs off after practice. And if I catch anybody sassin' a teacher, cheatin' on test, or skippin' class, I'll run ya off the team. Understood?" They nodded their compliance.

He turned and chalked up another command: *Good haircuts.* "No ducktails. And no hair hangin' in your eyes." He pointed to one of the boys in the front row who had closely cropped hair. "Stand up." The boy stood up compliantly. "Everybody get a good look. That's what I want on each of you before the week's out." A murmur rumbled through the bleachers, with the exception of the one boy who just sat down, basking in Pete's approval.

Pete ignored the groundswell of discontent and turned again to the chalkboard: *choir.* The word stood alone, cryptically, without negatives or qualifiers. He explained: "And I want everyone goin' out for choir."

The boys looked at him quizzically, and one of them raised his hand. "Ya mean, singin' kind o' choir?"

"Singin' kind," Pete answered. A few of the boys put down their notebooks and looked at each other in dismay. "I want you to be more a part of the school than just Friday-night football. And I want ya to realize ya got more than just a body that needs developin'. Besides, if you learn to sing together, maybe you can learn to play together."

Another boy raised his hand. "Those of us that can't sing, can we take woodshop instead, or maybe 4-H?"

"Those of us that can't sing," Pete paused and smiled, "are gonna learn."

After skull practice the boys went to the locker room to get adjustments made on their equipment. Then, for the second time that day, they took that long walk to the practice field, their football shoes tied together by the laces and slung over their shoulder pads.

After about twenty minutes of cal, Pete called to Byron. "Come over here, Jeffers." Byron put on his helmet and ran to the goalpost where Pete and the managers were standing. Hanging from the goalpost was a rope tied to an old tire. "I want you workin' today on your accuracy. Billy, get behind the tire." Pete rifled a spiral through the tire and into Billy's arms. Billy lobbed it back.

"Thread the needle," he said as he tossed the ball to Byron.

Byron took the ball and fired it at the tire, but it went wide a few feet to the left.

"You're not followin' through," Pete said. "Watch." He slowly went through the throwing motion without the ball, making sure he extended his arm and his fingers toward the target. "You try it." Byron planted his left foot and went through the motion. "Again," Pete said. "Follow through this time. Extend that arm." Again the boy pretended to take the snap, drop back, and throw. "With the ball this time." Billy lofted the ball to Byron, and the young, good-looking quarterback drilled it toward the tire. The ball was off the mark, nicking the outer edge of the black rubber O and ricocheting into the grass. "Slow it down. We're workin' on accuracy, not speed." And for the rest of practice Byron concentrated only on that black circle of rubber dangling from the goalpost.

Pete turned his attention to the rest of the boys. "We're gonna forget about offense for a while and concentrate on fundamentals—blocking and tackling. Get in two lines. I want one of you runnin' with the ball and the other one stoppin' him."

The boys scrambled to take their respective places. Pete handed the football to the first boy in line and blew the whistle. The defensive player threw himself at the ball carrier but just managed to get his arms around him. He held on and eventually downed him, but only after a gain of seven yards.

"You're arm-tacklin'. If you're gonna stop the ball carrier at the line of scrimmage, you gotta put your shoulder into him." Pete walked through the motion. "Put a helmet in his numbers, understand?"

"Yeah," the boy answered.

"Take a lap." The boy looked at him, puzzled. "Now." The boy took off running. Pete turned to the one next to him. "You understand?"

"Uh huh."

"Take a lap." He asked the next boy, Willie D., "Do you understand?" The boy froze, afraid that if he said anything he would be sentenced to the same fate. "Well, do you?"

The boy nodded his head vigorously. "Yes, I do, sir. Yessir."

Pete smiled. "Good."

He gave the ball to the next person in line. The boy gave a head-and-shoulder fake and skirted around the would-be tackler, leaving him in the dirt.

Pete extended him a hand: "Don't look at his head or his shoulders. Look at his gut. He can't fake you with his gut. Okay, next."

The next boy in line received the football. He faked right and cut back left. The defensive player crossed his legs on the fake and twisted off balance as the ball carrier cut past him.

"You crossed your legs. Never cross your legs. Move them laterally, like this." Pete demonstrated the movement. "Once you cross your legs, you're beat. Okay, let's make this a little more interesting and put in a blocker." Pete moved a boy between the ball carrier and the tackler. He blew the whistle. The blocker fended off the tackler, and the runner breezed by him, untouched.

"No, no. Here, watch." He moved the tackler to the side and gave him his glasses, then removed the whistle from around his neck and threw it to Billy. He got down in a three-point stance and squared off against the blocker. "Anytime you're ready, Billy."

Billy blew the whistle, and Pete shot out of his stance like a sprinter from his starting block. There was a crack of shoulder pads, Pete hitting the blocker and throwing him to the side in one motion. Then he wrapped his arms around the ball carrier and slammed him to the ground. A hush fell over the squad.

The fumbled football rolled to a stop near Cheetah's feet, and he casually bent down to pick it up. The circle of onlookers watched with their mouths agape as the runner struggled to get up.

Pete sprang to his feet, eager to go again. He pulled a boy by the jersey and set him in place: "Block." He looked around for another volunteer. "Gimme a ball carrier."

Terror shot through Cheetah, and he shoved the pigskin into the stomach of the boy next to him. The boy's eyes widened. A radius suddenly cleared around him. Billy blew the whistle, and Pete surged forward. He knocked the blocker into the ball carrier and stacked them on top of each other like cord wood.

Pete dusted himself off, put his glasses back on and then his whistle. "Everybody got that?"

A chorus of voices ascended from the field: "Yessir!"

5

While the boys showered, Pete drove home to see Beth. His arms, face, and neck throbbed with sunburn. His eyes were tired and dry and stung when he closed them. "Hi, hon," he said as he opened the screen door and kissed her on the cheek.

"You look beat."

"I am."

"I'll warm up your dinner."

"I ate with the team, didn't I tell ya?"

"No. Wasn't much of a dinner anyway."

He looked into the saucepans on the hot plate. One was filled with water and three hot dogs; the other with pork and beans. He dug a fork into the beans and sampled them, then speared a hot dog and bit off the end.

"How was workout?"

"Hot."

He laid his glasses on the end table and plopped onto the couch, exhausted. He placed a thumb and finger on his eyelids, rubbing them gently in slow circular motions. Underneath those lids he could feel every grain of sand, every spore of pollen that had collected there during the day.

"I saw a washing machine advertised in the paper."

"New or used?" he asked as he kicked off his shoes.

"New, but it was on sale."

51

"How much?"

"Seventy-nine dollars."

"You know we don't have that kind of money." He stretched out on the couch and closed his eyes.

"I thought we could put it on credit."

"When two-a-days are over, I'll check around for a used one."

He slept over two hours. During that time Beth took the opportunity to write to her mom, telling her about Pete's job and their new home and what it was like living in a small town. And she wrote about their eccentric landlady, who Beth believed was just a lonely person who had been lonely for too long. When she finished, she sealed the envelope and set it aside. She looked at Pete, still sleeping on the couch. She picked up a *Better Homes and Gardens* magazine, one that she had read before, and leafed through it mindlessly. She put it down, looked at Pete again, then pulled a book of Emily Dickinson's poetry from the shelf and cuddled up with it for a little companionship. The poem she read was one of her favorites:

> *If I can stop one heart from breaking,*
> *I shall not live in vain;*
> *If I can ease one life the aching,*
> *Or cool one pain,*
> *Or help one lonely person*
> *Into happiness again*
> *I shall not live in vain.*

Beth paused over the words, feeling a certain kinship with this shy poet whose life had consisted of such small ambitions and such simple prayers.

She put the book down and picked up a notebook, where she began scribbling her thoughts and playing with them until they finally fell into a few loosely rhyming couplets. When Pete awoke, she put her notebook away. He rubbed his eyes and looked at his watch. "What time is it?" He reached for his glasses.

"Little after ten."

"They'll be horsin' around till midnight if I don't get back." He sat up, bleary-eyed, and put on his shoes. He kissed her on the cheek. "I'll stop by in the mornin' after practice."

Driving into the school parking lot, Pete turned off his headlights, noticing that the lights to the gym were still on. He checked his watch.

In Pete's absence, Cheetah stood at the blackboard doing an impression of him. All the boys were gathered around, nodding obsequiously to his instructions, now and then raising a hand with some inane question or comment. On the board were written:

> *YES SIR, SERGEANT WILLIAMS, SIR*
> *NO CUSSING, except . . .*
> *BALLET*

"And I want each of you gettin' a little, pink tutu and goin' out for ballet—"

"He's coming!" shouted Hoot, who was keeping watch from the window at the top of the bleachers. The boys skittered around like cockroaches on a waxed floor, stepping into each other and over each other on the way to their cots.

"Cut off the light!"

Somebody pulled the handle on the fuse box, and the gym went suddenly black. A few seconds of silence ensued until a voice in the dark remembered: "The blackboard. Get up and erase it, Cheetah."

"You're closer."

"It's not my handwritin'."

There was a rustle of bedsheets and a thudding of feet on the floor. Just then the door opened and the ominous figure of their coach filled the doorway. Pete groped along the wall until he found the fuse box. The light revealed Cheetah erasing the board with his pillow, which he had successfully done with the exception of the last word. Immediately he turned and shielded himself with the pillow. He stood there in his underpants, his ribs sucking in the skin around them.

"Up kinda late, aren't we, John Henry?" asked Pete, as the boys snickered into their pillows.

"Must o' been sleepwalkin', Coach."

"Well try walkin' on back to bed." Cheetah looked over his shoulder to the last line on the chalkboard. "Sometime tonight," said Pete.

"Yessir." Cheetah backed up to the board, brushed it clean with his underwear, and hurried back to his cot.

Pete turned off the light, undressed, and crawled into his cot. He wound a clock, checking it to make sure the alarm was set, then put it on the floor.

The next morning it went off at 7:30. He picked up the clock and looked at it. "Rise and shine, boys. Breakfast in thirty minutes."

Their bodies were sacked away on the cots, dead weight, like bags of cement, their muscles stiff and sore from yesterday's workout. They stretched and groaned as they pulled their legs out of bed. Byron's feet slapped onto the cool hardwood floor; Billy's dangled from the edge of his cot.

Byron looked at him, expressionless. Billy looked back. Their hair was unkempt and their faces lined from the hard night's sleep. For a few seconds they just sat there, staring at each other. Then Byron flopped back on his cot. Billy jumped down and reached over to muss what little hair Byron had left. "Let's go, Tiger, up and at 'em."

The morning calisthenics were excruciating. Each exercise sent skewers of pain deep into their muscles. None of them had felt this sore in all their lives. When cal was over, Pete hoisted Billy onto his shoulders, and the manager tied the tire to the horizontal beam of the goalpost. Billy jumped down, and Pete waved for Byron.

"Today we're gonna have ya throwin' at movin' targets." Billy pushed the tire, and Pete threw the football through the swinging circle. Hoot caught the ball and threw it back.

"Ready?" asked Billy as he lifted the tire over his head. Byron nodded, and Billy shoved the tire off on its pendulous course. Byron cocked his arm and fired, but the target sailed by untouched. "Come on, Byron, you can do it." Fibber, who was standing nearby, echoed Billy's encouragement.

Pete left them so he could run the other boys through a rigorous routine of blocking and tackling drills. In the background Cheetah could be heard calling out, "I will not say 'yeah,'" each time he lapped the field. Pete had forgotten to tell him how many laps to run so he just kept lapping the field. To get Pete's attention, each time Cheetah passed by he enunciated a different syllable: "*I* will not say 'yeah'" . . . "I *will* not say 'yeah'" . . . "I will *not* say 'yeah.'" Each time he hollered out the team snickered, but Pete was so intent on the drills the boys were working on that he didn't notice him.

At the end of practice a whistle sent a ragged row of linemen sprinting down the field. Another sent a row of ends. Another, a row of backs. There was another whistle. And another. And another. The boys were holding their sides, panting for air and feeling as if they were going to pass out. Cheetah stumbled across the finish line, puffing out in breathy syllables, "I . . . will not . . . say—" And he dropped to his knees. "—yeah.'"

Pete called out to a tiring wave of lineman whose legs had turned to lead. "Come on, boys, you're doggin' it. Don't let up, don't let up."

After the workout the managers pulled boxes of game uniforms out of the equipment cage and took inventory.

"What are these?" asked Pete.

"Game uniforms," said Billy. "School couldn't afford to replace the ones we had, with the war and all, so for the last few years we been usin' SMU's hand-me-downs."

Pete picked up a jersey. It was well-worn and patched and had a red background and blue numbers. "They're not even our colors."

On the last workout of two-a-days the warm-up exercises sharply contrasted with those just two weeks previous. The side-straddle hops were brisk and in sync, the push-ups were executed with resolve, and the leg lifts didn't drag, not even Willie D.'s. The drills were enthusiastic. The blocking was solid. The tackling was head-on and brutal. Hoot and Billy stood at the goalpost, working with Byron on his passing drills. Billy gave the tire a push, and Byron spiraled the football straight through the moving O and into Hoot's waiting arms.

At the whistle they all lined up for windsprints. With each ensuing whistle they shot out of their stances and raced downfield. Whistle after whistle, they pushed themselves, reaching into their lungs for a second wind. And they ran, without letting up, thrusting their chests in front of them as they crossed the finish line.

Pete blew a final whistle, and the two grueling weeks of two-a-days were over. "Good workout, boys. Hit the showers."

They all let out a roar of approval as Billy and Hoot ran to meet them with a wooden case of Coke bottles, each bottle wrapped in tape and filled with water. "Swell goin', gang," said Billy. "Way to hustle, Freight Train." They took the bottles and poured them on their heads, letting the water cascade over their faces and down their necks.

6

School started on a warm, humid September morning. The air was tainted with the acrid smell of stiff, new clothes absorbing first-day-of-school sweat from the four hundred students gathered on the front lawn. When the bell rang, those students funneled through the center doors: freshmen, sophomores, juniors, seniors, and this year's McKinney Lions.

Their first class of the day was choir. The teacher's name was Maybelle Holden, a sparrow of a woman. Her voice was clipped, fluttering sometimes in frustration over a slow-learning student but never fully taking flight in anger. She was a nervous woman by nature, as if a tentative bird, wary of where it stepped. She was especially nervous today. Today enrollment for her class had swelled unexpectedly from a manageable thirty-two to an unwieldy fifty-nine, the additional twenty-four voices descending upon her in one fell swoop from the football team.

She squeezed them onto three rows of risers, spending the better part of the hour sorting them out, arranging the altos on one end and the sopranos on the other. Most of the football team fell into a vocal no-man's land somewhere in between.

"We'll start with something we all know," she announced with chirping optimism. As she played the prelude

on her piano to the national anthem, several of the boys
looked worried, unsure whether they remembered the words
and even more unsure whether their voices could rise to the
occasion.

Oh, say can you see
by the dawn's early light . . .

The voices clearly grated against the punctilious teacher,
and her trained ear searched the crowded risers for any errant
notes. She arose from the piano, leaving them unaccompa-
nied. The choir faltered, but a wave of her hand revived them.

O'er the ramparts we watched were so
gallantly streaming?

The closer she came to them, the more she winced as she
homed in on the flat note. It came from the right side of the
risers.

And the rocket's red glare,
the bombs bursting in—

"Stop. Stop." She waved down the choir, and the voices
trailed off into silence. "You there." She pointed to Hoot.
"You were flat."

"No, ma'am, couldn't've been me. I was just mouthin'
the words."

She eyed him suspiciously, then turned her gaze on
Cheetah standing next to him.

"I was mouthin' 'em too."

At the same hour, during his off period, Pete drove to
Kincaid's Hardware on the town square. When he entered the
store, he saw one of the last vestiges of a bygone era that had
stubbornly resisted the pull of the twentieth century. There
was no linoleum; only narrow lengths of plank flooring that
strained under the browsing weight of its customers. There

were no modern displays; only pigeonholes of oak, segregating everything from sixteen-penny nails to cotter pins. There were no oscillating fans; only an antiquated system of pulleys that twirled the blades of ceiling fans in lazy circles. There was no cash register; only a counter worn dark by the commerce of practical things, a pad, a pencil, and the *McGuffey* arithmetic shelved away in Kincaid's turn-of-the-century mind. Pete wandered through a maze of hardware aisles before he finally found Kincaid in one of them, sweeping.

"Afternoon, Mr. Kincaid."

"Hello, Mr. Williams."

"Hope I'm not catching you at a bad time."

"Nope."

"Since you're treasurer of the school board, I thought you would be the likely person to ask." Broaching the subject of money brought with it an awkward pause. "I was wondering if there might be any surplus in the school budget. Boys could sure use some new equipment."

"And the teachers could use a raise."

"I won't argue that," Pete said, smiling. "It's just that we've had to make-do with SMU's hand-me-downs for some time now, and well, they're pretty wore out; they're not even the school's colors."

"Cheaper changin' the school's colors than buyin' new uniforms."

"If we could just afford some better helmets."

"It's not in the budget."

"What *is* in the budget?"

"The coach's salary."

And that slowed the conversation down considerably. Pete regrouped his thoughts. "We're not talkin' about a whole lot of money—"

"The school district is out of money, Mr. Williams. We can't afford chin straps, let alone helmets, let alone entire uniforms. And if I did have it, I wouldn't send it your way."

Pete looked at him incredulously. "What?"

"I can't help a Yankee."

"A *Yankee?* How far north is Kansas?"

"North enough. I won't do anythin' to hurt ya—got nuthin' again' ya personally—but I won't do anythin' to help ya neither." He paused a beat and added: "Unless'n, o'course, yer wantin' to buy some hardware; I can help ya there."

"It's not in my budget." And he turned to walk away.

Late that night Pete sat up reading a book on the T-formation, but his thoughts kept traipsing back to Kincaid's store like a short-changed customer. Beth lay in bed next to him, asleep. He tried to get his mind back on strategy. Between now and next Friday night, he had to come up with a game plan. On the nightstand lay the sports section of the newspaper: "LIONS TO CLAW OUT SEASON OPENER WITH SHERMAN'S BEARCATS." He bit his nails as he studied the book. The boys were coming along, growing stronger and more determined with every day, but he didn't have a chance to scout the Sherman team, this being their season opener too, and he didn't know what to expect. He hoped for the best, but he feared it could make the burning of Atlanta look like a wiener roast.

He finally returned his football book to the shelf when his eye caught the title on the spine of another book: *Huckleberry Finn* by Mark Twain. He pulled it out, mused over it a moment, then put it with his notebooks on the nightstand.

The next day, in the cafeteria, Pete pulled up a chair beside Gill. "When you're first learnin' to ride a horse, and you fall off," said Pete, "what do you do?"

"If you fall off?"

"Uh huh."

"Ya git back on."

"Why?"

"Well, 'cause if ya don't do it right away, ya prob'ly never will."

Pete handed him his copy of *Huckleberry Finn*. "I want you to get back on that horse."

"I don't rightly know what you're gettin' at, Coach."

"You tried to put a saddle on American literature, and you got bucked off. That's all, just got bucked off. Happens to a lot of people. Don't walk away from it. Pick yourself up, dust yourself off, and get back on that horse."

Gill took the book. "I'll try."

Pete got up and patted him on the shoulder. "We're gonna miss ya tomorrow night."

"Gonna miss bein' there."

The next day Pete had all the players wear suits to school. Another one of his rules. The collar on Cheetah's neck chaffed him, as did the whole notion of dressing up for a football game. He came into Miss Caulfield's sophomore English class, adjusting that collar and straightening his tie. As he passed her desk, she casually looked up over her glasses, then went back to reading her book. The sight suddenly registered, and she looked up again, pulling her glasses farther down the bridge of her nose. Cheetah sat in his desk, and once he got settled, looked up to catch her staring.

"Mornin', Miss Caulfield." He ran his hand self-consciously over the sides of his new haircut.

"Good morning, John Henry."

Then Byron came in, also wearing a suit. Her eyes followed him to his desk. He sat down and noticed her staring.

"How are you this mornin', Miss Caulfield?"

"Fine, Byron, thank you. Special occasion today?"

"It's game day."

"Coach makes us wear 'em," explained Cheetah.

"He does?"

"The haircuts too," he added.

The seat between Byron and Cheetah belonged to Billy, but it was empty. He was trying to catch up with Kathy in the hall. The between-class crowds were thinning out, everybody hurrying to make it to their rooms before the bell rang. Billy picked up the pace to reach her before she slipped into Pete's American history class. He just wanted to get her attention, to see her face, her smile. The perfect opportunity came when a kid running to class bumped into her, knocking her books to the floor. Billy hurried to her side and bent down to help.

"Hiya, gorgeous."

"Oh, hi, Billy."

Once she had gathered the books in her arms, Billy stood up. She was still on her knees when she looked over to see him smiling at her. For Billy, it was a moment to treasure—the halls were empty, and there he was, alone with the girl of his dreams. Then Kathy stood up, towering over him.

"Thanks for the help."

"Shoot, it was nuthin'."

"I'd stay and talk, but I'll be late for class."

"Yeah, me too."

"Okay. Well, bye." And she drifted toward her class.

"So long," he said, waving.

She waved back. "I like your suit."

"Thanks."

The tardy bell rang, and Pete stepped into the hall to close the door to his class. She slipped in while Pete called out, "Hurry, Billy; you're late." He picked up his pace and started running down the hall, his street shoes sliding to a stop at Miss Caulfield's door. He adjusted his tie as he entered the class. "Sorry I'm late."

Miss Caulfield looked over her glasses and started to scold him, but with uncharacteristic restraint she gathered in her words and held them. Billy glided to his desk and sat down. Cheetah and Byron both looked at him, but he acknowledged neither of them. He was on cloud nine, and he didn't want anybody bringing him down to earth. He opened his notebook and, lost in a daydream, began sketching Kathy's name on his paper.

7

The trip to Sherman was a bumpy one, the old school bus taking the back roads, swerving occasionally to miss a chuckhole or a jackrabbit frozen in the glare of its headlights.

When they finally arrived at Sherman Stadium, it was brimming with locals who swallowed up the small group of McKinney fans who had showed up. Pete looked up in the stands and located Beth, who raised her hands to him with her fingers crossed. A few rows down, his eyes found Murphy, who gave him a thumbs-up. The McKinney fans who weren't there listened to the game over the radio, mostly to see if the new coach was going to pan out.

Grouped around a wooden Philco on the window sill of Cheetah's front porch were a dozen elderly pensioners, leaning forward, a few cupping their ears to hear the play-by-play coverage: "Bearcats on the twenty-yard line . . . Quarter-back takes the snap . . . hands off to—NO—fakes the handoff and bootlegs around right end. He's at the fifteen . . . the ten . . . the five . . . TOUCHDOWN! Sherman takes a six-nothing lead."

Uncle Clyde turned his pipe over and tapped out the old tobacco over the porch rail. "Sounds like the new coach is fixin' to git hisself some experience with a capital E."

"Point-after is good," broadcast the announcer. "Sherman, seven; McKinney, nothing."

As the Lions and Bearcats thrashed it out, Cheetah watched the fur fly from a fifty-yard-line seat on the McKinney bench next to Willie D.

"Think he'll put us in?" asked Willie D.

"I wouldn't bet your last cigarette on it."

And then a new thought flashed across Willie D.'s mind. "What if somebody gets hurt?"

Cheetah looked down the pine bench at the other boys sitting there. "Gonna take eleven somebodies gettin' hurt 'fore they get down to us."

The big gains that night were all made by Sherman, but almost every one of them ended in a fumble—eight in all, with credit going to the defense. In fact, Sherman's fumbles were what kept McKinney in the game. Going into the fourth quarter, the score was 12–7, Sherman.

It was third down and long yardage for McKinney as the referee spotted the ball deep in their own territory on the fourteen-yard line. Byron looked to the sidelines for a play from Pete, who signaled him to kick. Byron looked puzzled and motioned for him to repeat the sign. Pete repeated it, and Byron went slowly to the huddle.

On Cheetah's front porch the old men were calling out plays. They each had their favorite.

"Third and eighteen, we're gonna need to go deep, Coach."

"Button hook."

"Fake long and throw a screen pass to Jones."

"End over the middle."

The announcer picked up the action as the McKinney squad broke huddle. "The teams line up, and Jeffers drops back in—what's this?—punt formation? The defense hurries to adjust."

Billy ran to Pete and tried to get his attention. "What are you doin', Coach—"

"Not now, Billy—" said Pete as paced down the sideline, waiting for the ball to be snapped.

"But, Coach, it's only—"

"Third down!" hollered Clyde. "We're kickin' on third down?! What in tarnation—"

"There's the snap," said the announcer. "And the kick."

Uncle Clyde came uncorked. "Kickin' on third down! What kinda harebrained strategy is that?"

After the kick, boos rose from the small but stalwart band of McKinney fans. The McKinney bench looked over at Pete in disbelief. "What's the matter?" he asked. "What's everybody booing about?"

"It was third down, Coach," said Billy.

"*Third down?* I thought it was *fourth* down. It wasn't fourth down? Why didn't you tell me?"

"I tried to."

Pete slapped his forehead. The defense played as valiantly as they could with only a minute left, but the Bearcats ran out the clock, and the game ended in still another McKinney defeat.

The next morning in the barber shop the Saturday edition of the *Daily Courier Gazette* was folded over to the sports' page: "LIONS PUNT AWAY OPPORTUNITY TO WIN." The sound of scissors was drowned out by the snippy comments about Friday night's game.

"They could've won that game."

"If they had someone else callin' the plays."

"Somebody with a little experience."

As the men in the barber shop were getting their hair trimmed, McKinney's Newsome Stadium was getting a trim of its own. Pete had a hoe in hand and was working off his frustration by hacking away at the weeds. Murphy drove by on his way to get a haircut and saw him. He started to stop but drove on to the barber shop instead. He walked through the door of the crowded shop, and the conversation suddenly stopped.

"Mornin', Dale," he said to the barber.

"Mornin', Murph."

"Passed by the stadium on the way over. Coach was working by himself tryin' to get it ready for this week's game. Whaddya say a few of us go by and give him a hand?"

"Coach that punts on third down dudn't need a hand, he needs a foot—right square in the seat of his pants," said one of the men in the barber chair.

"A bus ticket out o' town, if ya ask me what he needs," said the man next to him.

"He just lost track of the downs, that's all," said Murphy. "Simple mistake."

"Stupid mistake."

"The job opened up a month ago, and I didn't see *you* standin' in line to take it; didn't see any o' you standin' in line to take it."

"I hear his strategy for this week's game is to kick on second down."

"That oughta catch the defense off guard."

"At this rate, by the time we start playin' conference games we'll be puntin' on first down."

"Now we can sit here like a bunch a buzzards around a ditched cow, waitin' for it to die," said Murphy, "or we can help git the cow out o' the ditch. What'll it be?"

There was a long silence, and then Murphy told the barber, "I'll come back midweek." He opened the door, then paused in the doorway and turned. "Twelve to seven. That's still the closest we come to a win in over two years."

Murphy drove to Newsome Stadium to help Pete with the field. After filling a wheelbarrow with the weeds Pete had dug up, Murphy rested on the handle of his rake. Pete continued chopping weeds. "I don't know what I was thinkin'. Stupid mistake. Stupid. Great way to start the season—"

"Ain't gonna do no good rehashin' it all. Someday you'll look back and laugh at it."

"When?"

"It'll be a while, I 'spect." He looked at Pete and tried to hold back his smile. "Prob'ly a good while."

8

McKinney football hadn't exactly been front-page news the past two years, and the *Gazette* couldn't justify a sportswriter on the payroll. Pete assigned the job to Billy, and the newspaper was only too happy to have the free labor. Sunday night the boy sat at a desk in his room, hunched over his typewriter, sweating a deadline. He stared at the white page, lingering over the one word that stood out in bold type: McKINNEY. With his index fingers he finished the headline: TO HOST ENNIS FRIDAY NIGHT. He mused a moment over the wording, then pecked at the keys again: "by Billy Button." And that seemed enough to get his creative juices going.

The next morning he stood outside Miss Caulfield's door, waiting for Byron. When he walked up, Billy handed him the article.

"You finished it, huh?" said Byron.

"Late last night. Let me know what you think."

"When do you need it back?"

"Before workout."

"Today?"

Billy nodded. "And check the grammar and all that stuff too, will ya? I don't mind lookin' stupid in front of a few friends, but I don't want to look that way in front of the whole town."

Gill stopped by his locker and talked with the two boys. Miss Caulfield, chalking an assignment on the board for the class, overheard them.

"Close game the other night," Gill said. "Couldn't get a ride, but I heard all about it."

"Wish you could've been there," said Byron, "I mean, on the field."

"We could've used you."

"Ya did alright without me."

"We missed ya anyway," said Byron.

Later that morning Miss Caulfield went to the office with a stack of papers in her hand and saw Gill in a chair, reading.

"Hello, Gill."

Gill looked up from his book. "Howdy, Miss Caulfield."

She began putting her papers in the pigeonholes that were the teachers' mailboxes. "What are you reading?"

"*Huckleberry Finn*. Coach gave it to me."

What he said registered with her, but she let it pass without comment. "Waiting to see Mr. Stedman?"

"Yes'm. Havta explain about missin' school; had to help Daddy shore up the barn."

Mr. Stedman poked his head out of his room. "Okay, Gill, I'm ready for you now. Come on in."

After Gill went into Mr. Stedman's room, Pete entered the office to check his mailbox.

Miss Caulfield handed him one of her papers. " 'Visitor Sunday' this week at my church, if you're interested. I'm inviting all the faculty. Didn't want to exclude anyone."

"No, I'm sure you didn't." Pete skimmed the notice, then folded it up.

She took off her glasses and turned to him. "High school is an impressionable time for young boys, Mr. Williams. The example we teachers set should be one of clear and uncompromising principles." She paused. "Church is where a person picks up those principles."

"I appreciate the—" Pete put the paper in his shirt pocket. "—the invitation."

At practice that afternoon Pete's whistle sent a defensive player into a head-on collision with a blocker and a ball carrier. When the boy with the ball got up, he tossed it to Byron, who was next in line. Cheetah stood opposite him, settled in a three-point stance, waiting for the whistle. When it came, he crashed into the blocker and knocked him aside, crouching in wait for Byron to make an evasive move. But Byron didn't make that move. Instead, he lowered his shoulders and plowed right through him.

"Way to lower that shoulder," said Pete. "Good hit."

The hit impressed everyone on the field. Except Cheetah. He got up slowly, humiliated by such a public defeat. The two joined the others who had already finished the drill. As Cheetah bent down to tie his shoe, Byron said to him, "Gonna have to be tougher than that to play here."

Cheetah charged and knocked him to the ground, his momentum thrusting his face within inches of Byron's.

"Tough enough for ya?"

Pete grabbed his jersey and pulled him to his feet. "You wanna fight or play football?" Cheetah stood silent and defiant. "Well?"

"Football," mumbled Cheetah.

Pete clutched a handful of jersey and pulled it to him. "What?!"

"Football."

"Then keep your personal problems off the field."

That night Pete had problems of his own, trying to field questions from an intrusive sportswriter from the Greenville newspaper. Beth, meanwhile, was busy setting the table. She had Spam frying in a pan and some macaroni with butter in a pot next to it. She motioned to him it was time to eat.

When he finally got off the phone, dinner was cold.

"I ran across an announcement in today's paper about the Poetry Club. They're having their monthly get-together Thursday night. It's open to the public, the article said."

"You ought to go."

"It's something I've always wanted to learn about. I do a little on my own, but I don't know if it's any good. Anyway, I thought I would go and see what it's like."

"I don't have anything going that night; I'd be happy to drop ya or you can take the car, whatever."

Beth started to vacillate. "They probably all have their degree."

"It's just a piece o' paper, Beth. Doesn't make a person better'n anybody else. I got one, and look at me."

Beth smiled.

He shoveled a forkful of macaroni into his mouth. "Goin' to college doesn't make ya smart. And not goin' doesn't make ya dumb."

Beth drove herself to the Thursday night meeting, which met in the library of the high school. She brought her notebook and pencil in case notes were expected to be taken or in case there was someone there who wanted to see her poetry. Ten women showed up, a good turnout in the opinion of the hostess. Beth was the only newcomer. She had thought there would be more, hoped there would be more. After all, it was open to the public.

The women sat in a circle of chairs. They were mostly Beth's age, but somehow they seemed a little older; their hair, a little nicer; their dresses, a little more stylish.

There was a reading of the minutes from last month's meeting at which the treasurer donated a volume of poetry to the library on behalf of the Club. "New business" consisted of a discussion about raising dues, which was resolutely motioned, seconded, and was passed unanimously by a show of hands. After the formalities, the hostess turned the attention of the group to Beth.

"So, you're the new coach's wife?"

"Yes."

"And you're from Kansas?"

"Illinois actually; Pete's from Kansas."

"Lincoln's state."

"Kansas?"

"No, Illinois."

"Yes," said Beth, her eyes growing hopeful. "They have a big exhibit for him in Springfield."

"And whom are you studying right now?" asked one of the other women.

"Whom am I studying?"

"What poet?"

"Well, I'm not really studying—" Beth began, "I like Emily Dickinson. I mean, I like the way she writes."

"She *has written a few* good things."

"Oh, she's written a lot more than that. I have all her poems. I've got them all in one book if you would ever need, like to borrow it."

The women in the circle cut their eyes at each other.

"I'm sure it will be a while before I get around to studying Dickinson, but thank you, anyway," the hostess said, feigning politeness as several of the women fought back their smiles. An awkward moment of silence spread over the circle.

"How about you?" Beth asked. "Who are you studying, now."

"Rilke."

"Rilke?"

"Ranier Maria Rilke. The German poet."

"I've heard of her, I've just never read any of her poems," Beth said.

The women cut their eyes toward each other and could no longer suppress their smiles.

Beth didn't let anyone see her poetry that night, which she clutched next to her side like a security blanket. No one asked to see it, and she didn't volunteer to show it.

Refreshments were served afterward. As Beth was getting a cup of punch, she overheard one of the women say under her breath to another: "She's not really one of us."

When Beth came home, Pete was at the dining table, reading an American history book in preparation for tomorrow's class. She quietly shut the door behind her. Pete looked up at her.

"How was it?"

"Okay." She put her notebook back on the shelf.

"Many people there?"

"Ten." She took off her shoes.

"Have a good time?"

"It wasn't—" She struggled with the zipper on her dress. "—what I expected."

"And what was that?" Pete got up to help her.

"Something different."

"That tells me a lot." He kissed her neck.

"I don't feel like talking. I'm tired. I just want to go to bed." And she walked out of the room.

The next afternoon Pete got Billy and Hoot out of class, and the three of them chalked the football field with powdered lime to get it ready for the game.

It was the first home-game, and the way the stands were filling up that night, it looked as if it were going to be a sellout. Seems everybody wanted a look at the coach. You start kicking on third down, and a certain reputation precedes you.

Beth sat with Ted, who had made repairs on the stands until just before game time and was still in his work clothes. Gill sat in the student section, his first chance to see the young Lions in action.

Pete gathered the boys underneath the stands and talked with them about a few last-minute details before he released them to do their warm-up exercises. As they took off for the field, Billy noticed Cheetah's jersey.

"Hey, Cheetah, wait up."

Cheetah stopped and turned. "Whaddya need, Button?"

"Ya got a rip in your jersey."

"I know," he said and started to leave.

"It's gotta be fixed."

"Don't worry 'bout it; he's not gonna play me anyway."

"Not my job to say who plays and who doesn't; my job's to make sure everybody's ready to play. So sit down and let me sew you up."

Cheetah complained but sat down anyway. Billy got a needle and thread out of the equipment box and started sewing the rip, every once in a while letting his needle get a little ahead of him.

"Hey, watch what you're doin'!" snapped Cheetah. "Ouch. I swear you're tryin' to stick me."

Billy tied off the loose end of the thread. "If I was tryin' to stick ya . . . I'd do this." And he stuck the needle in Cheetah's back end.

"Ow!" Cheetah shot to his feet.

"Now git out there and warm up with the rest of 'em."

The sun simmered on the horizon as the game got under way, its hang-over heat lingering long after dark. By the end of the first half the score was 6 to 0, Ennis's favor. The boys huddled around Pete underneath the bleachers. Hoot and Billy were busy giving them stubby Coke bottles filled with water, which they poured over their throbbing heads. The heat coming up from their jerseys was almost suffocating.

As Pete went over second-half strategy, Freight Train started writhing on the ground.

"What is it, Al? What's wrong?" asked Pete.

The halfback grimaced as he squeezed out the word, "Cramps."

"Managers, get 'im more water and some salt."

Hoot got the salt tablets from the equipment box. Al popped them into the boy's mouth and Hoot washed them down with a chug of water. As he did, Billy kneaded his muscles, working the cramps out of the boy's legs.

"Ow, ow, ow."

"Don't tense up," Billy said as he massaged the boy's calves. "Straighten out your leg."

Before long the cramps subsided, and the managers had him up and walking. Pete sidelined him the first part of the third quarter, just to be safe, but let him play the rest of the game. The second half proved to be a little cooler than the first, but a few of the players still almost passed out from the heat. Midway into the fourth quarter Pete pulled Byron out for a rest. Billy cleared a seat for him on the bench and got him a bottle of water.

"Freight Train's hittin' the line too early," Billy said. "He's there before the hole opens up. He's half a step ahead of his blocker."

"Should I have him start off slower?"

"No. When ya line up in the backfield, just move 'im back a yard."

"Okay."

The defense played a great game that night, holding the visiting team to just one touchdown. Late in the fourth quarter the Lions finally got on the scoreboard with a safety, the defense sacking the Ennis quarterback in the end zone. The final score: MCKINNEY 2—ENNIS 6.

As the teams mingled with each other and shook hands, Murphy and Beth wove through the crowd to find Pete.

"Almost," said Beth. "We were so close."

"Defense played a real good game, Coach," Murphy said as he patted Pete on the back.

"Doesn't do much good without an offense."

"Offense is only as good as its line; and the line could use a little gumption."

The next morning Pete slept in until Beth came and shook him. "Pete. You wanted to go to the barber shop this morning, remember?"

Pete groaned and rolled over. "What time is it?"

"Nine o'clock."

"It'll be too crowded."

"So."

"So I don't want to go."

"Why?"

"I don't feel like an earful of advice, and that's what I'll get at the barber shop."

"You really need one if we're going to church tomorrow."

"I just need a trim. You could give me a trim, couldn't ya?"

Sunday morning Pete and Beth arrived at Miss Caulfield's church. They came at 10:45, thinking the service started at 11:00, but it had started at 10:30. As they entered, Pete was still wearing his hat. Beth scolded him with a look, then whispered, "The hat."

Reluctantly he complied, revealing a few bare patches where Beth's scissors had come too close. Entering the foyer, they were greeted by two ushers who were hard at the work of fellowship, smiling, shaking hands, and making latecomers feel a little more welcome than they generally wanted to feel under the circumstances. During the offertory hymn, one of the ushers led them down the aisle and squeezed them into a worn wooden pew near the front. You had to come early if you wanted a good safe seat in the back, which was where Cheetah sat, along with his mother and a few of the pensioners. As Pete settled into the pew, his eye caught Elaine

Caulfield's across the aisle. He nodded a greeting, and, almost imperceptibly, she nodded back.

The minister read from the *Revised Standard New Testament,* which had just been published that year. The members who were used to the more familiar cadences of the *King James* were convinced that the change of translations would lead to liberalism and wholesale waywardness, but the minister wasn't quite so convinced and read from it anyway.

"John, chapter twenty-one, beginning at the fifteenth verse: 'When they had finished breakfast, Jesus said to Simon Peter, "Simon, son of John, do you love me more than these?" He said to him, "Yes, Lord; you know that I love you." He said to him, "Feed my lambs." A second time he said to him, "Simon, son of John, do you love me?" He said to him, "Yes, Lord; you know that I love you." He said to him, "Tend my sheep." He said to him the third time, "Simon, son of John, do you love me?" Peter was grieved because he said to him a third time, "Do you love me?" And he said to him, "Lord, you know everything; you know that I love you." Jesus said to him, "Feed my sheep."'

"May God richly bless the reading of His Word. And may He remind us that this greatest commission ever given a disciple was given to the disciple who deserved it least. To Peter. Yes, Peter, the Rock, that Gibraltar of a man who crumbled the night of our Lord's arrest.

"If you recall, three times that night he denied Jesus. And now three times Jesus commissions him to 'Feed my sheep.' It was Jesus' way of saying, 'I still believe in you, Peter. In spite of your failure, I still want to use you to build my church.'

"'Feed my sheep.' With those words Jesus handed Peter some pretty big shoes to fill. But had Jesus not given him a second chance, Peter would have never had the opportunity to grow into those shoes.

"The Law shows us how greatly we have failed; Grace

shows us how greatly we have been forgiven. It was Grace that gave Peter a second chance. It is Grace that gives all of us who have ever failed a second chance—whether we are merchants or mill workers or ministers. However great the failure, the Grace of God is greater."

After the sermon a final hymn was sung and the ushers dismissed the pews by rows. The line threaded through the front door, where the minister stood and greeted people as they were leaving. Finally he shook Beth's hand; then Pete's.

"Reverend Chattsworth."

"Beth Williams, and this is my husband Pete."

"The coach?" asked the minister, and Pete nodded. The minister shook his hand more vigorously. "Heard a lot about you." He bent forward and whispered. "Kicking on third down. That's kind of like dismissing the congregation before taking the offering."

Pete laughed. "I guess it is."

"I did that once, first time I preached here."

"You don't say."

"It's the gospel truth."

"Not that I was doubtin' ya, Reverend."

And then the minister laughed.

"Welcome to McKinney, Coach and Mrs. Williams. And welcome to this church. Good to have you here. Real good."

9

The losses to Sherman and Ennis were both nonconference ones, and the general feeling, at least around the barber shop, was that the real season didn't start until the first conference game.

Which was Greenville.

Home of the blackest dirt and the whitest people.

And, according to preseason polls, home of the seventh-ranked team in the state.

Monday, talk about the upcoming game permeated the lunchroom. Gill sat with some of the football players, eating a sack lunch filled with four peanut butter-and-jelly sandwiches. Billy and Hoot bounded past them to get Pete's attention.

"Hey, Coach. Wait up." He and Hoot ran to Pete as he returned his tray to the dishwasher. "Found a way to get the word out about Friday's game."

"You'll love it," said Hoot. Both were so excited they could hardly contain themselves.

"What is it?"

"Come on. We'll show ya," said Billy.

They led him to the teachers' parking lot, where on top of his car were tied two speakers.

"Well, whaddya think?" asked Hoot.

"Swell, huh?" said Billy.

"What is it?"

"Give us the keys to the Gray Goose, and we'll show ya," said Hoot. Pete burrowed into his pocket and tossed him the keys. The boys jumped into the car. Hoot started the ignition, and the car jerked into reverse as he tried to back it out of the parking space. He wiggled the stick on the steering column, then popped the clutch. The car lurched forward and died.

"You do know how to drive, don't you, Hoot?"

He started the engine again, wrestled with the gearshift, and eased off on the clutch. The transmission stuttered at first but eventually smoothed out.

As they drove around the parking lot, Billy announced over the speakers: "The Lions will be playing Greenville this Friday night, so everybody come out and show your support for the team. Game time: seven-thirty at Greenville Stadium."

Pete was up late, worrying about that game. He pored over the scraps of paper strewn on the dinner table, lost in a scribble of X's and O's. Beth came over to rub his shoulders. She could feel the tension as she kneaded his muscles. He studied the scraps of strategy littering the table, trying to piece together some sort of game plan.

"It's going to be tough game, isn't it?"

"Seventh in the state. We're gonna get killed."

"Nobody'll be expecting you to beat a state-ranked team."

"I'm not worried about winnin'; I'm worried about the boys gettin' hurt."

The phone rang, and Beth answered it. It was for her, but it was a short conversation and within a minute she was back rubbing Pete's neck.

"That was Lynell Jeffers."

"Byron's mom?" asked Pete.

"Mm hm. Since you would be riding over on the bus with the boys, she thought I might need a ride and asked me to go over with Bob and her. Said her son couldn't say enough about all the good you were doing the team."

"He might change his mind after Friday night."

Pete was at school early the next morning, holed away in his office, still scribbling game strategy. Slender fingers of steam from his coffee cup slowly ascended to touch his forehead where they began to unravel the tangle of anxious thoughts that bound him. He had scouted Greenville the week before and, after seeing their tenacious defense, thought the best strategy might be to punt on first downs. Of course, there wasn't much job security in that type of coaching strategy, and he dismissed the idea in a rumple of paper.

At noon he went to the boiler room in the school's basement to eat lunch with Ted Murphy. He chewed on a white-bread baloney sandwich, watching intently as the janitor drew a play on his lunch sack.

"We called it the 'Sideline Phantom.' Coach pulled three men out but just sent two back in. The other'n stood on the sidelines, his feet just barely in bounds. Nobody noticed him; thought he was out of bounds with the rest of the team. When the ball was snapped, he tore out. Quarterback hit him goin' long. Faked the defense right out of their jocks."

"Thanks," said Pete as he folded up the sack and put it in his pocket. "I need all the help I can get."

"Don't suppose you seen the Greenville paper?" the janitor asked. Pete shook his head. Murphy pulled the newspaper from a cubbyhole in a battered rolltop desk. "Came out yesterday." Pete picked up the article and started skimming it. "Read on down," Murphy said, pointing to the last paragraph.

"So don't expect much of a contest, because the McKinney Lions couldn't beat a good junior-high team." Pete pondered the article for a few seconds and then asked, "Do me a favor, will ya, Ted?"

"Sure."

"Drive over to Greenville and pick me up twenty-five of these." He reached for his billfold.

"That Yankee money's no good here," Murphy said, waving him off with his hand. "Anyway, don't 'spect ya got much leeway on a coach's salary."

"No, not much."

Ted delivered the newspapers that afternoon. Before practice, Pete cut out the articles and taped one to each boy's locker. The extra copy he taped on the mirror.

When the boys filtered in to suit up, one by one they noticed the article. As they read it, the mood shifted from the usual kidding around to a quieter, more introspective one. Some felt a tinge of embarrassment. Others, humiliation. Still others, outrage.

As the boys were suiting up, Billy knocked on Pete's door.

"Come in."

Billy shut the door behind him, a sprig of anger growing out of his hurt. "Why'd'ya rub their nose in the newspaper like that?"

"At some point, Billy, they've got to look themselves in the mirror, and each one of 'em has got to ask himself a real important question: 'What am I made of?' If they don't, other people will answer it for 'em—the way that sportswriter did."

"I just don't think the message was that clear to 'em, that's all."

"Then I'll spell it out for 'em at practice; fair enough?"

The feelings that washed over the boys in the locker room were dredged up later on the practice field.

"Hold it, hold it, hold it!" Pete stormed over to the two boys in the blocking drill. "Your job is to protect the quarterback. If you don't dig in and get tough, the Greenville defense is gonna take off his head and drop-kick it into the nickel seats. You want that to happen?!"

"No, sir."

He looked at the other blocker. "*You* want that to happen?!"

"No, sir."

Pete turned to give his glasses and whistle to Billy. The faces of the blockers fell.

"I'm gonna rush in to get the quarterback. It's your job to see that I don't."

When Billy blew the whistle, Pete split the two blockers as though they were bowling pins and sacked Byron. As he got up and dusted himself off, he said: "I guess that sportswriter was right." He reached to get his glasses, and Freight Train spoke up.

"He wasn't right." Pete turned to face the boy. "We may not be the best team to ever suit up for this town—" He paused to collect himself. "—but we're not what he said either." There was a tense silence. Nobody spoke. Nobody even moved.

"Prove it," said Pete.

Picking up the gauntlet, the two boys spread out to entrench themselves around Byron and dug their cleats into the ground. Pete returned his glasses to Billy. When the whistle blew, he smashed into the one boy, knocking him back a yard, but the boy held his ground. The other blocker backed him up and kept Pete from penetrating. The more vigorously he tried to get to Byron, the more vigorously they blocked. The harder he hit, the harder they hit back. He wheeled around to make a final charge when one of the boys hit him low and the other hit him high, knocking him flat on his back.

He lay there for a moment with the wind knocked out of him. Then, pulling himself up to rest on his elbows, he took a shallow breath, just enough to exhale four words: "That's more like it."

What the Greenville sportswriter had said cut deep into each boy, and, though he never said as much, into Pete as well. Try as they might, they couldn't get those words out of their minds.

But it was those words sinking in that brought from the very depths of them a new resolve. At the end of practice, Pete blew his whistle for sprints. First was a row of linemen, shouting, "Beat Greenville!" as they raced downfield. Another whistle, and the ends shouted, "Beat Greenville!" Another whistle signaling the backs, and another enthusiastic "Beat Greenville!"

When they hit the showers, the exhausted boys stood under the spray, letting the cool rivulets of water stream down their sun-baked bodies. Byron was first out of the shower and stood in front of the mirror, combing his hair. His eyes fell on the Greenville article in the lower corner. He looked back at himself in the mirror, then he tore it off, wadded it up, and threw it in the trash.

The enthusiasm of the players was infectious, breaking out in banners throughout the halls of McKinney High. *Go, Lions. Devour Greenville. Seventh in the state, don't even rate. Go, fight, Win tonight.* The talk around the lockers was how much the team had improved over the past six weeks . . . how the offense was beginning to gel . . . how the season was just really starting.

The Greenville game brought the whole school together, not just the football players. It was all everyone talked about in the halls that week. Through those bannered halls streamed the children of businessmen, mill workers, and farmers. The farm kids comprised the frayed hem of the county; their clothes, plain and worn and smelling pungently of yesterday's chores. The Mill District kids were a cleaner lot but a cruder one; the boys tended to smoke more and the girls to get pregnant sooner. The city kids—sons of merchants and daughters of professional people—were generally the leaders of the school, involved in all the activities. The one thing that brought them all together and erased the distinctions existing between them was Friday-night football. The pithy ribbons they all wore pinned to their shirts. The spirited cheers they all chanted into the night air. The alma mater they sang together at the end of the game. Those wooden bleachers were the place where they were all equal, if only for a few autumn evenings.

Those spirited hallways were empty now. It was the end of the day, and Murphy was making his custodial rounds, emptying the trash in each room, sweeping the floors, and sponging down the blackboards. When he came to Miss Caulfield's room, he was surprised to find her still at her desk, working.

"'Scuse me, Miss Caulfield, I'll come back later."

"No, it's all right."

"Y' sure?"

"No bother, really," she said.

Murphy emptied her trash and noticed a number of streamers advertising the upcoming game. "Lot of excitement about Friday's game."

"Hm?"

"The Greenville game. Lot of excitement about it." He took a streamer out of the trash and showed her.

"I'm not much of a fan, I'm afraid."

"A shame; great sport, football." Miss Caulfield gave no reply, and Murphy started scrubbing down the blackboard behind her. "You heard of the 1909 team, haven't ya?"

"You can't live in McKinney and *not* hear about it."

"I was on that team." Miss Caulfield turned in her chair and looked at him over her reading glasses. "Oh, I know I don't look like much of an athlete, but before my knees wore out, I was a pretty fair runner; only sophomore on the first string."

"And what did football ever give you besides bad knees?"

Murphy squeezed out his sponge in the mop bucket.

"Don't rightly know; never thought about it." They both went back to their work; she to her textbook, he to his blackboard. "Got a lot of memories, so I 'spect that's somethin'." He paused. "Somethin' else. It gave me a dream."

"A dream?"

A wistful memory of the boy he once was came back to him, the boy with a wiry physique and good knees. "I dreamed about playin' football in college when I graduated, somewhere that had a big stadium, lots of green grass, full of people, band playin' and all that. . . ."

"Where did you end up going?"

"Nowhere. Papa needed me to help get in the fall cotton, and back then, when the cotton was ready, ya got your books from school and stayed home till after the harvest. Did your pickin' by day; done your book learnin' at night. When the cotton started comin' in, I had a chance to make a few dollars pickin' for the neighbors. Ended up followin' the cotton crop all the way to Oklahoma. Money in my pocket and the world was my store."

"Did you go back, to school, I mean?"

"Got so far behind I didn't think I could ever catch up. I kick myself now. But when you're seventeen, you don't look down the road—just at the step in front of ya. And you put your foot down, and ya wake up the next mornin' and put the other'n down, and the other'n, and one day ya look up and ya got a family, kids, regular job . . . and ya can't go back and pick up those dreams you left behind. Never really gave it much thought before ya asked, but maybe that's why the memories mean so much—they were the part of the dream I got to live. Reckon that's so, Miss Caulfield?"

She smiled kindly. "I reckon that's so, Mr. Murphy. I reckon that's so."

After a week of rigorous preparation, the day of the game finally arrived. The boys all wore suits. Their coats were roomy and their ties looked as if they had come from deep in the forgotten recesses of their fathers' closets. But there was something different from the way they looked last week. The clothes were the same, but somehow *they* were different. You could see it in the set of their jaws . . . hear it in the tone of their conversations . . . feel it in the air around them as they clumped together in huddles of two or three in the hall or as they sat together in the cafeteria.

The auditorium was decorated for the pep rally with rolls of butcher paper, mottoed with blue and gold tempera paint. The fight song blared from the small but spirited band, and the yell leaders kept everybody on their feet, clapping to the hard-driving beat. The three girls on stage wore white, pleated skirts with matching sweaters, each emblazoned with a big blue M in front. Three boy yell leaders complemented them, wearing similar sweaters with white trousers.

A sentinel of teachers stood along the walls, keeping watch over the crowd. Among them was Elaine Caulfield. With a certain professional detachment she looked over the student body that swayed to the pounding waves of music. Sitting toward the back of the auditorium was Gill Thompson. He was on his feet with the rest of them, responding to the yell leaders' megaphoned commands. But all the while, he felt a certain detachment of his own, like a graduate coming back for homecoming, belonging there but not really belonging.

Across the auditorium Miss Caulfield saw Pete dressed in a suit, his hands taking refuge in its pockets. Her attention was diverted to the stage when the music teacher introduced a choral arrangement of "America the Beautiful." The football players in the front row of the auditorium stood and filed out of their seats to take their place on stage with the rest of the choir.

Her interest piqued, Miss Caulfield listened as the voices unfurled in patriotic salute to their country. The crescendo of voices was met with an outpouring of applause. Miss Caulfied's eyes fell casually upon Pete to find him clapping and beaming over his boys. Suddenly drawn out of detachment, she looked back at Gill, and she continued looking until the applause ended and the audience was seated.

After the pep rally, she returned to her room. There, a couple of cast-iron radiators stood dormant under the windows, and a freshly erased blackboard stared blankly down rows of vacant desks. A great emptiness came over her as she sat there in that classroom, alone with her thoughts. And with that emptiness came a feeling she didn't have very often, a feeling that maybe she had been wrong.

She slowly opened the lower desk drawer and pulled out last semester's grade book. *American Literature. Spring Semester*. She opened it, and her finger moved down the alphabet until she came to *Thompson, Gill*. Her eyes followed the horizontal line of indictments that the literary world had marshaled against him. An F stood in the final column. She inched open the top drawer and took out a pencil. She touched that F with her eraser. It was a timid touch, like a leper venturing through the doors of a temple, this shrine to education where no one dared set foot. The gummed sole of her eraser shuffled over that sacred ground, a step forward, a step back. Before long, the F was just so many soft filings to be whisked away with a sweep of her hand. And, in a quiet moment of conscience, Grace triumphed over Law.

She got up from her desk and walked to the locker room in search of Pete. It was such a foreign place to her, that hollow-sounding room where there were no desks, no books, no pictures on the wall—only the heavy smell of sweat mingled with analgesic balm. The boys were lined up at the equipment cage getting game uniforms issued to them by the managers. They all became quiet when they saw her.

"Can I help you, Miss Caulfield?" asked Byron.

"Is Mr. Williams in?"

"I'll take ya to his office." He escorted her to a 10 x 10 office where Pete was culling out several pieces of paper from the heap on his desk and putting them in a clipboard. Byron rapped on the door frame. "Someone to see ya, Coach."

"Miss Caulfield," he said, shooting to his feet. Byron closed the door as he left. Suddenly self-conscious in her presence, he said, "Excuse the mess. Day of the game things get pretty hectic around here." He started to clear a place for her to sit. "Here, sit down."

"I can't stay." A pregnant pause labored between them, Pete feeling like an inadequate midwife to her thoughts. "I just wanted you to know—" She paused a beat. "It's a good thing, what you're doing with the boys. I've noticed a big change. They're working harder in class, more polite. They're an example to the rest of the school."

"They're good kids; just needed a little spit and polish here and there, that's all."

There was another contracted pause before she took a deep breath and pushed out the words.

"About the talk we had—"

"I was wrong to come bargin' in like I did, bull in a china shop. It's just my way; I didn't mean anything by it."

"You were right." And that stopped Pete cold. "Gill deserves another chance."

He paused to frame his response carefully. "I wouldn't want you goin' against your principles, Miss Caulfield, and I mean that sincerely."

"If our principles—" She corrected herself. "—no, if holding on to our principles becomes more important than holding on to people, people like Gill Thompson, well, then maybe we need ask ourselves why we have principles in the first place." She paused for a breath. "I want to give him a make-up exam."

"When?"

"Seems a shame that he's missed so much already—first two games of the season, choir. I was thinking today."

Pete flung open the door and hollered, "Byron!"

"Yessir."

"Go to the office and get Gill out of class!"

Yes, sir!

Pete reached out and shook her hand. "Thank you, Miss Caulfield . . . for Gill's sake."

When Gill arrived at her room, she seated him in the front desk, gave him a pencil and a sheet of paper, and explained about the exam. On the blackboard she printed the test questions:

1. Who wrote *Huckleberry Finn*?
2. Why did Huck run away from home?
3. Whom did he meet . . .

That afternoon Hoot and Billy drove Coach's car through McKinney, announcing the game. They drove around the town square:

"The McKinney Lions will be traveling to Greenville tonight—"

They drove through the Mill District:

"—Kickoff's at seven thirty—"

And they made a special trip to the Thompson farm. The car ambled down the road with its loudspeaker disrupting the quiet of the country air. Mr. Thompson was repairing a fence and paused to take notice. The kids all ran to get their mother from the kitchen.

"—So everybody come out and support the team—"

Billy paused until Mrs. Thompson came to the porch.

"—Captain for tonight's game is Gill Thompson."

10

Greenville lay thirty miles east of McKinney and boasted a population of seventeen thousand. By the time the school bus arrived there, the sun had dipped below a distant hill. As they shouldered their gear and got off the bus, the McKinney Lions gaped at the stadium, its silhouette looming against the ripening pink of the North Texas sky.

For many people in Greenville, that concrete stadium was their cathedral and Friday nights, their Sabbath. Businesses closed early in preparation for the weekly pilgrimage to that shrine, and for those faithful fans the ecstasy of those nights was a near-religious experience.

Billy and Hoot had done such a good job of getting the word out that some twenty-five hundred McKinney fans caravaned over Highway 24 for the game that night. Beth came with Byron's parents. Ted Murphy drove over with some of his old teammates. As the fans trickled in, the McKinney squad was deep within the catacombs of that colosseum, putting on their padded armor a piece at a time, slowly, deliberately, pensively. By the time all the fans had arrived, the stadium was overflowing with seventy-five hundred people.

When the Lions had finished dressing, Pete gathered them all together. "Okay, boys, listen up." Their cleats chattered nervously over the cement floor as they settled onto the benches. He stood in front of a blackboard, holding a piece of chalk, tumbling it over and over in his hand as if it were a rosary. In his other hand was a program. "Here's what we're up against, boys. Center, 225 pounds. Right guard, 215. Left guard, 205. Right tackle, 210. Left tackle, 195. You're not going to whip 'em standin' flat-footed. Your only chance is to keep 'em off-balance; a lot of cross-blocking, a lot of pulling and trapping. Four-point stance, linemen, don't forget. We're gonna lean on ya tonight, Gill; gonna lean heavy. If ya need a breather, let me know." Gill nodded.

"Any questions?" Pete asked, but there were none. "One more thing 'fore we go out. I want ya to know, I don't believe what that sportswriter said. I don't think you believe it, either. Problem is, lot of people in those stands do. I can't do anything to change that; they make me stand on the sidelines." He paused a moment as he looked around the room. "*You* gotta be the ones to change their mind." He paused to survey their serious faces, then turned to Billy. "You got anything to add to that, Billy?"

The boy thought a second, then said to the team, "Let's go out there and give that sportswriter somethin' to really write about."

With a clap of his hands and a flinty scraping of cleats, they were off to the playing field, determined to prove themselves, to the fans, to Coach, and to that Greenville sportswriter. When they stepped onto that field, six poles of light stared down on them, as though a pantheon of gods were peering down upon a duel of Titans and mortals. Below the lights, an incline of fans were on their feet, cheering for the gladiatorial contest to begin. The young warriors from McKinney found themselves overcome by the spectacle. They had never played in such a stadium before, or in front of such a crowd. For a moment the roar of that crowd went mute. All they could hear was the beating of their hearts in their helmets. All they could see was the blur of overhead lights in their eyes.

Gill seemed to be the only player who wasn't overcome by it all and he tried to bring his teammates back to reality. "Hey, come on, we gotta game to play! Snap out of it! Let's go!" he shouted as he slapped them on their shoulder pads and helmets.

The pounding of their hearts gave way to the pounding of bass drums; and the blinding lights, to the array of color in the stands. Byron took the lead, running to the visitors' sidelines, his teammates following close behind.

Representing McKinney, Gill walked to the center of the field with the officials and the three Greenville captains. When he did, Murphy, who was sitting immediately behind Beth, squinted down at him. "These eyes are gettin' too old. I could swear that was—"

"—Gill Thompson," Beth said, completing his sentence.

"I thought he—"

"He was. Miss Caulfield gave him a make-up test." She smiled. "He passed."

"Why that ol' softy," said Murphy.

The field was lush, smelling richly of freshly mowed grass, and etched meticulously with increments of powdered lime. Greenville got the nod to make the call as the official sent a silver dollar glinting into the air. Heads it was, and they elected to receive.

Greenville took the ball on the kickoff and cut a swath through the turf to the McKinney forty-two-yard line. The Greenville fans jumped to their feet and cheered. On second down the defense clogged the line of scrimmage, causing the fullback to stumble for a gain of only one. Now it was McKinney's turn to stand up and cheer.

Mr. Stedman, the superintendent, rose to his feet, but his cheers were drowned out by Reverend Chattsworth's, "All right, Lions! Way to hit! Way to put a helmet in those numbers!" Willard Kincaid stood next to him, clapping but not knowing quite what to make of this side of the Reverend, which he had not seen before.

On the next play the quarterback rolled out to pass, but Byron, playing defensive back, batted it down. Again, the McKinney fans rallied.

Bob and Lynell Jeffers stood next to Ted Murphy, and as the cheers died down, Bob leaned over to Ted. "Ain't no flies on my boy."

It was third and nine. Greenville faked the fullback up the middle and pitched out to the halfback churning up the field around left end. The play posted a gain of five, but it wasn't enough for a first. The Lions' cheering section went wild.

Kathy, Connie Sue, and Mary Ellen were jumping up and down, hugging each other. The students around them were hurling their fists into the air, cheering the team on.

Fourth down and four yards to go, Greenville elected to punt. The kicker sent the ball sailing into the night sky, where it dropped into the McKinney end zone. The official brought it out to the twenty-yard line.

Pete played his starters both ways, so when they lined up in a T-formation, they were still trying to catch their breaths from the last series of downs. Byron took command behind the center. Freight Train flanked the fullback on the right side. Byron motioned to him and said, "Back up." The boy stepped back a yard and then settled into his stance.

There was a long count—"hut five, hut six"—then the right side of the McKinney line exploded. Gill opened a hole big enough for a train to run through. Freight Train took the handoff and barreled through the opening. A linebacker got a hand on him, but that was all. Three defensive backs converged to stop him, but he slanted past them and laid track down the middle of the field. The entire stadium was on its feet: McKinney, in hysteric euphoria; Greenville, in stunned silence. Two of the defensive backs raced to catch him. He steamed past them to the fifty . . . the forty. . . . One of them made a desperate lunge, grabbing only air, which caused the other to stumble. It was open field from there on out. Thirty . . . twenty . . . ten . . . Touchdown!

The Greenville coach threw his clipboard to the ground and cursed the air. Pandemonium erupted on the McKinney side. A couple of the players ran off the field, and Billy ran to meet them, cheering them, rallying them, and following them to the sidelines. As Freight Train came off the field, Pete threw his arms around him.

"Way to run, Al! Thatta boy! Way to get the job done!"

The breathless boy took off his helmet and gulped down deep draughts of the heady night air. As he paced the sidelines to catch his breath, the McKinney fans continued to stand and applaud him. It was a mercurial moment of glory. Someday it would slip between the fingers of McKinney's collective memory, but for now, in the cupped cement hand of Greenville Stadium, his eighty yards of immortality was secure, secure and shining under the Friday-night lights.

Over the roar of the crowd Pete yelled to Billy: "We win this one, and you can have the game ball."

The pride of lean and hungry Lions huddled together. In their eyes was the frenzy of first blood; in their mouths, the foretaste of victory.

The kick for the extra point veered off to the right. HOME 0—VISITOR 6. The remainder of the half seesawed back and forth in a hard-fought defensive struggle, Greenville grinding out five first downs to McKinney's three. Gill was awesome defensively, sacking the quarterback four times, penetrating the backfield and breaking up a number of plays.

When the first-half gun sounded, the Lions ran off the field. Their locker room was a chaos of emotion.

"Anybody hurt?" Pete called out over the noise. None of

them were, but if they were, they were too pumped with adrenaline to feel it. "Gill, you doin' okay?"

"Yessir. Feelin' my oats," he said with a grin.

"Byron?"

"Okay, Coach."

"I look for 'em to key on Freight Train the second half," said Pete as he chalked a play on the blackboard. "If they do, we want to fake to him and run some options: 43 Belly, 44 Trap, or, if the linebackers are cheatin' up, Byron, hit the end comin' over the middle."

The haggard-looking starters hung on every one of Pete's words. Their uniforms were smudged with dirt, drenched with sweat, and smeared with grass stains. Blood seeped from cleat marks on several of their arms and legs. Pete put the chalk in the rail and turned to them.

"Boys, that was the best half of high school football I've ever seen." The boys slapped each other on the back and congratulated each other, but the noise quickly died down as Pete motioned for quiet. "Problem is, you gotta play 'em another half. And believe me, they're gonna have your number, they're flat gonna have your number. Right now their coach is chewin' 'em up one side and down the other. He's grabbin' 'em by the jerseys, shoutin' in their faces, tellin' 'em who they are—seventh in the state—and who you are— a bunch of cotton farmers that couldn't beat a good junior high team. They're gonna come out the second half, not to beat ya, but to humiliate ya. I don't know how you're gonna do it, but you gotta play better than you did the first half. You gotta play the best football you ever played in your life." He paused a moment, looking into their battle-scarred faces. He felt the emotion welling up inside him, but he fought it. "I'm proud of ya; want you to know that."

The second-half kickoff skittered sideways across the ground and was fumbled momentarily before the runner found the handle. One Greenville player tackled him, but three others piled on after he was down. The McKinney fans booed the referee.

Pete yelled to the official. "Come on, Ref, they're pilin' on!"

Cheetah jumped off the bench. "What're they payin' ya, Ref?" He turned to Willie D. "How could he miss that? He was right there."

But the officials ignored the taunts coming from the McKinney sidelines. On the next play, a Greenville lineman smashed Gill's face with an elbow. He fell to the ground, his nose gushing blood. Again the McKinney fans booed the referees for not throwing a flag. The official called time-out, and Pete ran with the managers to help him. Cheetah stepped over the sidelines and onto the field, challenging the offending player.

"You wanna fight? Hey, you, I'm talkin' to you! You wanna fight? Come and get it! Come on!"

Billy ran to Cheetah. "Off the field," he said, waving him to the sidelines. "We're gonna get penalized, now come on, get off the field."

Cheetah ignored Billy and continued to taunt the Greenville player. "Right here waitin' for ya! Right here, right now!"

Pete and Hoot bent over Gill. "You okay, Son?"

He nodded that he was. Pete left Hoot to attend to him and stormed over to an official. "Come on, Ref, where's your flag?"

"No flag 'cause there's no foul."

"Whaddya mean, no foul? Every eye in the stadium saw it."

"Mine didn't, and they're the only ones that count."

Pete pushed a finger in the man's chest. "If any of my boys get hurt 'cause you're not doin' your job, I'm gonna—"

A Greenville player put his hand on Pete's shoulder, pulling him back. Cheetah bolted from the sidelines and connected with the Greenville player's jaw. Both benches emptied onto the field. Volleys of threats were exchanged, along with a few punches.

As Beth watched anxiously from the stands, Murphy cheered them on.

Eventually the referees, assisted by the Greenville police, restored order. Fifteen yards were marched off against McKinney for unsportsmanlike conduct. Boos again arose from the McKinney section. The penalty proved to be too much yardage for the Lions to reclaim, and they were finally forced to punt.

The next series of downs Greenville started double-teaming Gill, and soon the momentum shifted. They ground out gains of three and four yards a carry until they finally pushed the ball in for a TD. The point-after was good. HOME 7—VISITOR 6.

The second half was largely a ground battle rather than an aerial campaign. It was trench warfare, the Greenville coach hoping to wear down the smaller McKinney line. Gill took a beating, as did the rest of the McKinney linemen, but they held their ground, and by midway into the fourth quarter the score remained unchanged. As time wound down, the real enemy became the clock. Cheetah stood tensed on the sidelines, watching that clock, gnawing his fingernails to the quick.

With two minutes left to play, McKinney had the ball deep in their own territory. Murphy muttered to himself in the stands. "Now. Run it now."

A screen pass netted them five yards, and the fullback up the middle added another two.

Murphy was sweating it out by now. He cupped his hands and called out. "Come on, Coach, run it now!"

It was third down, and the Lions needed three yards to keep the drive alive. Byron looked to Pete on the sidelines, who sent in a lineman. As they huddled up, the lineman revealed the play: "34 slant right."

Byron added, "On one. Quick count, so everybody get set." They broke huddle with a clap and dug into their positions. Gill steeled himself for the block. The Greenville guard and tackle keyed on him, and the linebacker positioned himself to rush. Byron moved into position to take the snap. "Hut one." Gill charged like a bull broncking out of a chute, but the Greenville line was ready for him and dropped the ball carrier just over the line of scrimmage.

The officials brought out the chain and measured the distance for the first down. Fourth and one. The clock showed just under one minute to go in the game. Cheetah's nails were all nubs. Pete signaled a time-out.

The two teams ran to their respective sidelines, ushered off the field by the euphoria of their fans. Both bands struck up their fight songs, and the stadium shook. Beth shouted through the makeshift megaphone of her rolled-up program, "Come on, Lions, you can do it, you can do it!"

Down on the field, Pete waved Byron to the sidelines. He took his clipboard and began to sketch the play. "Sideline Phantom. Send Wilemon, Smith, and Freight Train out of the game. When I send Wilemon and Smith back in, make sure Wilemon drops off the line and fills in the vacant slot in the backfield." The boy nodded. "Defense should all be playin' up, anticipatin' the run."

Byron sent the three players to the sidelines. They huddled around Pete as he went over the play.

Billy rounded up the bench warmers: "Everybody off the bench and crowd the sidelines." Soon, all thirteen of them were standing next to Pete.

Two of the boys went back in, while Freight Train took off his helmet, as if resting, and knelt on one knee just inside the out-of-bounds marker.

Seeing that McKinney wasn't going to punt on fourth

down, the defensive line closed ranks. The linebackers filled in any gaps. The defensive backs moved up to stop any short pass that might be thrown over the middle.

The fans were on their feet, both sides cheering their litanies of encouragement: *Hold 'em, defense. Let's go, Lions. Push 'em back, push 'em back, waaaay back. You can do it, Lions!*

As the Lions broke their huddle, the Greenville coach spotted Freight Train on the sidelines putting on his helmet. Quickly he counted the number of players coming out of the huddle. Two, three . . . five . . . eight, ten. One short. He squinted at Freight Train again, noticing this time that he was in bounds.

The Greenville coach yelled to his defensive secondary. "Get back!" He dropped the clipboard and ran down the sidelines, waving them back. "Get back! Get back!" But the roar of the crowd was so great that none of his players could hear him.

"Hut one, hut two . . ."

The coach yelled more frantically, pointing to the far side of the field. One of his defensive backs saw the commotion on the sidelines, followed the coach's hand, and spotted the McKinney player near the sidelines. He tore off on a ragged footrace across the field.

"Hut three." The center hiked the ball. The lines collided in a thunderous crack of shoulder pads. Byron pivoted and faked to the halfback who plunged into the air over Gill. The Greenville linebacker threw himself into the vaulting halfback and pushed him back to the line of scrimmage. By this time Byron had backpeddled into a protected pocket. He drew back his arm and launched the long bomb. The defensive back ran desperately to the other side of the field, but Freight Train had twenty yards on him. He streaked down the sidelines and without breaking stride caught the ball on the Greenville forty. The McKinney fans went hog-squealing-wild. Thirty . . . twenty . . . ten . . . TOUCHDOWN!

Beth threw her arms around Lynell. Behind them, you could see in Murphy's eyes the flame of an embered memory fanned to life from hands that couldn't stop clapping. The point after was good. HOME 7—VISITOR 13. And that's what the scoreboard read when the final gun sounded.

As the McKinney fans cascaded down the bleachers and flooded the field, Pete ran to catch up with the Greenville coach who had gone to center field to retrieve the game ball.

"Wait up. Hey, Coach, wait up!"

The Greenville coach saw him approaching but turned to walk away. Pete caught up with him and cut off his path of retreat. "I believe the winner gets the game ball."

"It's our ball." He started walking away, but Pete cut in front of him.

"It's our win."

"Balls are hard to come by."

"I've got a promise to keep with that ball. Either you're givin' it to me, or you're gonna take your second beatin' here tonight."

Pete clenched his fists and moved toward him, but Willard Kincaid stepped between them. "We'll send you another ball to replace it." The Greenville coach hesitated. "It's not worth fightin' over. We'll buy you another one," urged Kincaid. Reluctantly the man gave in and handed him the ball. Kincaid gave it to Pete, and when he did, it was as though he had taken a stone off the wall of bitterness that still stood between parts of the South and the rest the Union. Before either of them had a chance to say anything, though, the McKinney players flocked around Pete, lifting him onto their shoulders. And as they carried him off the field, he tossed the game ball to Billy.

11

The horizon splayed the sun, giving light for the morning chores and color to the weathered grays that made up the Thompson farm. The oldest of the Thompson girls had just skimmed the cream from the raw, warm milk with a hand separator and was bringing it indoors where one of the younger boys was waiting to churn it into butter. In the kitchen the plump wood stove sat agitating a considerably smaller pot of coffee. Next to it lay a skillet crackling with pork rinds. Mrs. Thompson was grinding dried kernels of corn into meal, which she added to the flour to make it stretch further. Another of the girls took the mixture and made biscuits out of it. When the pork rinds were crisp, Mrs. Thompson spooned them out and used the remaining grease to make gravy.

Soon the smells filtering from the kitchen enticed the rest of the family away from their morning chores. They each took their seats, waiting eagerly for the biscuits to get done. When they were, Mrs. Thompson put them on a platter and placed them on the table. Gill, meanwhile, was still asleep on one of the pallets on the living room floor, and since he was the oldest and biggest of the Thompson kids, his absence from the table left a gaping hole.

"Where's Gill?" Mr. Thompson asked his wife.

"He didn't git home from the game until late."

107

"Go git 'im, Joey."

"Let 'im sleep," said Mrs. Thompson. "He's plumb wore out."

Her husband conceded. "Pass the gravy, Kay Lynn."

He tore open his biscuits and covered them with gravy. Through a mouthful of the mixture he asked, "They git beat again?"

"No, thirteen to seven, they won."

A shuffling sound coming from the doorway caused everyone to look up. Filling that doorway was Gill, bleary-eyed, his hair matted down, his nose scabbed and puffy from the night before.

"Good morning, Gill," said his mother, and all the kids in their own way echoed the greeting.

He blinked a few times to get his bearings. "Mornin'." He moved to the table stiffly and eased himself into his chair with a groan. As he did, the other kids grimaced.

"Don't just sit there gawkin'," said Mrs. Thompson, "give the boy some food."

Later that morning Mr. Thompson was in the barn, pitching forks of hay to the two dairy cows that were tethered there. He put his pitchfork down and slowly straightened himself, his hand rubbing the small of his back as he sat down on a bale of hay. He reached under a nearby bale and pulled out a pint of whiskey, taking a swig. When he heard the barn door creak open, he spun the top back on and furtively let the bottle slip from his hand to the back side of the bale.

"Finished with the gate," said Gill.

Mr. Thompson reached for the pitchfork and used it to push himself up. "M' back give out on me," he said, partly to justify his sitting down and partly to prepare the boy for his next statement. "Gonna need your help gittin' the cotton in, ya know that, don't ya?"

There was a long pause.

"The team's countin' on me."

"Well, I'm countin' on ya too."

"I'll make up the work after football—"

"What's football ever gonna do for ya? It gonna get ya a job, put food on the table?"

"Coach thinks football could maybe get me a scholarship to college."

"College? Now whaddya gonna do with all that learnin'? Read, write, and figure—that's all a man needs to git 'im by."

Gill looked at him and tried to explain his feelings, but feelings weren't something he was used to explaining, especially to his father. "I wanna do more than just get by. I think about things sometimes, things I wanna do with my life."

"Kickin' a pigskin around a cow pasture? You call that doin' somethin' with yer life? What yer *gonna* do with yer life is help git the cotton in. Ya don't need a college edgycation to understand that, do ya?"

"No, sir."

So Monday morning as the school bus made its usual rounds, it stopped by the Thompson farm but without picking up its usual load of Thompson kids.

As soon as the dew was off the cotton, the Thompsons were all out in the fields, straddling the rows of long-stem plants with their gunnysacks to their sides. They plucked the white fluff from the clinging grasp of the bolls that held them, careful not to pick any leaves because they would stain the cotton and lower its grade when they went to sell it at the gin.

Mrs. Thompson brought a number-2 washpot full of beans and placed it under the wagon with a cloth over it to keep the bugs out. Next to it she placed a Dutch oven full of soda biscuits. She worked beside them until late afternoon, then she went back to the house to get dinner ready. The rest of the family, except for the younger children, worked until dusk.

As the sun slipped below the horizon, it took back the

color it had earlier given. Once again the Thompson farm became a somber collection of grays. Gill was the last one in from the fields, and the nearer he got to home, the darker those grays became.

The next day after workout the boys tumbled into the locker room, their faces parched from the sun, their sweaty jerseys almost suffocating them. They couldn't peel off their uniforms fast enough to get into the showers for a bellyful of cool water. One by one they came dripping from those showers and took a towel from the stack that Billy was guarding.

Byron came out of the shower and reached for a towel. "I wonder where Gill was today."

"I 'spect he's still recoverin' from Friday night," Billy said. "He got worked over pretty good."

Cheetah came out of the shower and grabbed two towels.

"Eh, eh. Just one," admonished Billy. Reluctantly he put the other towel back.

"Hey, Button," hollered Hoot from the equipment cage, "where're the ankle wraps?"

Billy turned and pointed. "The white metal box in the corner there."

With Billy's attention diverted, Cheetah plucked another towel from the stack.

"Find it?"

"Yeah," replied Hoot, lifting the wrap from the box. "Thanks."

Cheetah had dried himself off and was combing his hair in front of the mirror, one towel wrapped around his waist and one draped around his shoulders. Byron had just finished showering and was toweling off next to him when Billy came by, paddle in hand. When he saw Cheetah with two towels, he became incensed. He pulled the towel from Cheetah's waist, drew back to get a full swing, and swatted him.

"Ow!" Cheetah whipped around, gritting his teeth.

"One towel. You know the rules." Billy shook his paddle at him. "I don't know how you got it, but it better not happen again."

Cheetah grabbed the paddle from Billy's hand. "This is what better not happen again—you little chimp." Cheetah threw the paddle to the floor. The affront jarred Billy, but he picked up his paddle and left the room without incident.

"You didn't need to say that," said Byron.

Cheetah shot him a hard glance. "Nobody asked you."

Walking home from Monday's practice, Cheetah stopped at the Texaco station. He dug in his jeans for a nickel and dropped it in the slot of the rectangular drink-machine standing near the door. He raised the cover, pulled out a Grapette, and pried off the cap in the bottle opener. He took a swig, then walked off.

A couple of older boys sitting on the curb watched him walk away. They sat in their jeans and T-shirts and leather jackets, cigarettes dangling from their lips.

"Looky there, Joey. It's the famous McKinney pine rider."

"Watch out for those splinters, Cheetah. That bench can be pretty rough."

The two boys snickered. Cheetah exploded. He hurled the bottle at them, and it crashed into the curb, sending slivers of glass everywhere. The boys shielded themselves, then shot to their feet. Cheetah plowed into them, knocking both boys to the ground.

From the window the gas station attendant saw the three of them fighting and dialed the police. The fight had been going on for several minutes when a squad car screeched to a stop in front of the station. The boys scattered in three directions, knocking over trash cans and jumping over fences to make their escape.

The heavyset policeman jumped from his car and ran

after one of them, but he couldn't keep up and had to abandon the chase. He plodded back to his car, panting, and asked the attendant, "You get a good . . . a good look at 'em?"

"Only one I saw good was that Brown kid."

"Him again, huh?"

That night at Cheetah's house his mother, Nadine Brown, was busy getting dinner ready. The chairs surrounding the dinner table were an odd assemblage, like those who were seated in them. A ladderback with a cane seat peeking through to the floor. A Victorian chair, its darkly stained baroque carvings looking incongruous next to its cushion, which had grown little goatees of cream-colored stuffing. A cherry-wood Duncan Phyfe with a mismatched leg grafted to one corner. The chairs were orphans she had adopted from the secondhand store, as was the china. The only two pieces that matched were wedding dishes, having survived the years but not very gracefully.

A mound of potatoes rose from the base of a white, ceramic bowl, yellow streams flowing from its peak and a big spoon buried in its side. A wicker basket cradled the buttermilk biscuits that were swaddled in a faded floral napkin. Beside it sat a sunken tureen of cream gravy. At the other end of the table, tempting fingers of steam ascended from a platter of fried chicken. The old men around the table sat impatiently waiting to eat. The youngest and most impatient was Sydney, who was mentally retarded.

Nadine looked over the table to make sure everything was on and then mumbled to herself, "Now where's Clyde?" Sydney pointed to the front porch. She opened the screen door to catch Clyde throwing a rock at a black boy walking across the street.

"Stop that!" she admonished. "Stop that right now! It's not right the way you treat them, Clyde; they're our neighbors."

"They're colored."

"Then they're *colored* neighbors, but they're still neighbors, and I won't tolerate yer treatin' 'em like that."

Cheetah came bounding up the porch steps with his uniform slung over his shoulder. "Howdy, Uncle Clyde. How's the Good Samaritan?"

"Supper's on," she said to Cheetah. "Hurry and worsh up."

At the supper table sixteen men bowed their heads for Nadine's prayer. As she prayed, Sydney reached for a crispy morsel from the chicken platter, but Cheetah looked up, giving him the evil eye, and Sydney withdrew his hand and bowed his head compliantly.

"—and we thank Thee, Most Gracious Heavenly Father for the bounty of which we are about to partake. Amen."

"Pass the corn," said Uncle Clyde to Cheetah and then muttered under his breath, "Next thing ya know she'll be takin' one o' them nigras under her wing and givin' him a seat at the supper table."

"I just might surprise you someday and do that," she said.

"Wouldn't surprise me none. Surprised ya hadn't done it before now."

One brittle, stick-figure of a man at the end of the table piped up, "Think you could dust yer broom somewheres else, Clyde? Fer once I'd like to get through a meal without your jaw flappin' in the wind."

Clyde was an inspector at the cotton mill, and due to his penchant for passing judgment, it was a job for which he was particularly well-suited. He had a wooden leg from "the Great War," as he liked to refer to it, and as a war-wise veteran, he had gotten into the habit of telling FDR, through the audience at the supper table, what he needed to know about the Germans if he wanted to draw a quick close to the war. As it happened, word never reached the President, and the war went on, in Clyde's opinion, a couple of years longer than necessary.

Now that the war was over, it left something of a hole in the evening conversation—a void which Uncle Clyde was quick to fill with diatribes about boll weevils, Yankees, or "coloreds," all encroachments on his life. Nadine wouldn't let him call them anything other than "colored" at the table, although on the porch as he sat in a rocking chair and mumbled into his pipe, he called them anything he darn well pleased.

Sitting opposite of Uncle Clyde was Sydney, fortyish, but nobody, least of all Sydney, knew how close to forty. A dumpy man, he always seemed to have his belt cinched too tight with an inordinate length of tired leather drooping from his buckle. He dressed himself, but he had the appearance of having been dressed by somebody else who didn't have the time. His eyes protruded to such an extent that you always thought he was excited about something. And usually he was. Clyde eyed Sydney with irritation as he noticed three bowls backed up at his place.

"Will ya pass the food, Sydney? Other people'd like to eat too, ya know."

While Sydney passed the food, Nadine asked her son, "Goin' to choir practice at church tonight?"

He swallowed his potatoes. "I know ya got yer heart set on me bein' a Gospel singer and all." He took a gulp of milk. "But I don't see the Lord dealin' me out that kind of hand." The glass clicked when he set it down. The only sound was the scraping of silverware against the plates.

"Sheriff came by a few minutes ago. Said you keep pickin' fights, he's gonna send ya to reform school."

Suddenly the silverware went mute.

"I don't pick fights, Ma—"

"A gentle answer turneth away wrath."

"I tried that holy approach once," he said as he chewed

on an ear of corn, "and got the tar beat out of me." Suddenly his attention became diverted. "Hey, somebody stop Sydney; he's hoggin' all the biscuits."

Cheetah excused himself from the table. He opened the medicine cabinet and dashed some of Uncle Clyde's green hair tonic into the palm of his hand and worked it through his short hair. He put up his fists as if he were a boxer posing for a photograph. He looked stern in his first pose and smiled in his next. When he did, he noticed a piece of corn between his teeth.

There was a loud honk from the driveway. "Yo ride's here, John Henwy," called Sydney.

Cheetah dug at the piece of corn with his fingernail when another honk sounded.

"John Henry!" hollered Clyde.

"Coming." There were a couple of short, impatient honks, which sent Cheetah breezing past the dining room, where he gave his mom a peck on the cheek, and went sailing out the door, singing, "Coming for to carry me home. Swing low, sweet chariot—"

He vaulted into the backseat of a yellow Chevy ragtop that had two slick-haired, leather-jacketed dropouts in front. The tires laid a streak of rubber in front of his house.

Cheetah slapped the driver in the back of the head. "I told ya to stop peelin' out in front of my house, Nub. My mom's ridin' me enough as it is."

"Okay, okay. Just tryin' out the new wheels and got a little carried away, that's all," he replied as he took a sharp turn and spun out around a corner. He put the car in first and popped the clutch, two of his tires screaming in protest against the asphalt.

"This a '38?" asked Cheetah.

"'39," the boy said proudly. "Only 28,000 miles; one owner."

"How much it set you back?" Cheetah asked.

"Hadn't bought it yet; still checkin' her out."

"How fast'll she go?" asked Cheetah.

"Go ahead, show him," said the boy in the front seat, smiling.

The driver tossed his cigarette and laid rubber in all three gears. On the open stretch of road ahead of them he opened her up, forty . . . fifty . . . sixty, the wind whipping over their faces, exhilarating them.

Then, from out of nowhere, they heard the sound of a siren. Nub looked in his rear-view mirror and saw the flashing red light of a rapidly approaching police car.

"I don't need this, Nub," said Cheetah. "I got my share of trouble with the law without you addin' to it."

In another part of town, Pete was at the supper table sketching out a new play on a sheet of paper in preparation for the next game. Beth was in the bathroom, hunched over the tub, washing out socks. The room was strung with a clothesline from which were hung her husband's underwear.

The phone rang once, twice, and Pete was so wrapped up in his work he was oblivious to it.

"I'll get it," Beth said, drying her hands on a bath towel. She pushed herself to her feet and got the phone. "Hello. Yes, he is. I'll get him." She put her hand over the receiver. "It's for you." He was still lost in his work, and she had to call again. "Pete, telephone."

"Who is it?"

"Reverend Chattsworth."

He got up, and she handed him the phone.

"Hello. I do, yes, Reverend. How are you tonight?" As the conversation continued, Beth went back to the socks soaking in the bathtub. She rinsed the soap out under the faucet and wrung them out before hanging them on the line.

Reverend Chattsworth tried to fill Pete in about Cheetah's past. "His daddy left when he was three. There's a lot of pain the boy's got bottled up inside. Between that and his mother's work with the pensioners, he's never had the home life most boys his age have had."

Pete listened as he watched Beth straining over the side of the tub, sweat dripping down her face.

"I just got through visiting with his mother," continued Chattsworth. "She was crying and pretty distraught. Sheriff told her if she couldn't handle her son, he was going to send him to reform school. She wanted me to help, but I think you're in a better position to do that than I am. In a lot of ways we're in the same business, you and I are, Coach Williams." He paused a couple of seconds, then continued. "Whatever you can do to keep him off the streets and away from the crowd he's running with, it would ease his mother's aching heart."

As Pete watched Beth string up the socks with clothespins, he noticed her wiping the sweat away with the back of her hand. "That's what we're here for," he said into the phone. "I will, yes. Good-bye."

He went into the bathroom and helped her pin some socks to the clothesline. "When I get a raise, whaddya say we get a new washer?"

"It's not the washer," she said, feeling like the limp sock she was wringing out. "It's you bein' gone all the time. And when you're here, your mind's in Sherman or Ennis or wherever this week's game is. You're either scribbling in your playbook or else talking on the phone all evening with people we don't even know."

"It's my job, Beth."

She took the socks from his hand. "Twenty-four hours a day?" She let the water out of the tub and walked into the living room to stand in front of the fan.

"I know it's taken a lot of time, but next year things'll ease up."

"What about *this* year? I need you *this* year. I need to talk about something besides football once in a while. I need a little companionship. When you're gone, you know who that leaves me with? Sue. And believe me, a little of Sue goes a long way."

"I'm sorry, sweetheart. I know it's been hard—"

She sighed as the fan revived her. "I know you've got a lot of work ahead of you, and what you're doing for all the boys is a good thing, I know that, I believe that. It's just that, just that I need you too."

The next day Pete walked with Murphy around the school grounds as the janitor speared bits of trash and put them into a gunnysack.

"He's a likeable kid, good sense of humor; just got a short fuse."

"I seen him fight before. One day after school, against a kid a lot bigger'n him. He's good. But ya gotta find some way to harness that fight. Ya don't need a maverick kickin' down the corral. Either gotta break him . . . or let him go."

"I can't let him go; it'd kill his mom. Help me, Ted."

"How?"

"Tell me how to break him?"

That afternoon before practice the football players were dressed in their school clothes and sitting on the bleachers in the gym for skull practice. Billy sat on the bottom row with Fibber sleeping on the floor next to his feet.

"Any word on Gill?" Pete asked.

"I talked with his sister this morning," said one of the boys. "She wanted me to get his books. Said his daddy needed him to help with the cotton."

Pete mulled the information over in his mind, tumbling the piece of chalk over and over in his hand as he did. Finally he said, "Okay, let's review what we covered last time. How can you win a game without scoring?"

Several of the boys raised their hands. Pete pointed to

Byron. "If the other team doesn't show up, you win by forfeit."

"Okay, what's another way?"

Byron raised his hand again, and Cheetah, sitting a row back, took the opportunity to taunt him. "Get two in a row right at McKinney High, and they retire your jersey."

"Pay attention, John Henry," corrected Pete.

"Yessir."

Pete pointed to one of the boys in the front row who answered, "By penetrations."

"That's right," said Pete. "Each time you cross the opponent's twenty-yard line with the ball, that counts as a penetration. Even if the score is zero to zero at the end of the game, the team with the most penetrations wins."

"Jeffers, any of this penetratin' that skull o' yours?" Cheetah whispered.

Hearing the remark, Pete charged up the bleachers in giant strides and picked Cheetah up by the shoulders. "If you're gonna play football here, Son, you're gonna listen when I talk, do you understand?" Cheetah froze and didn't respond. Pete shook him and raised his voice. "Do you understand?!"

"Yessir." Cheetah's face flushed with embarrassment.

Pete walked down the bleachers, every eye riveted on him as his steps echoed throughout the gym.

In the same gym that night Pete unlocked the door and flipped on the lights. He was followed by Cheetah, who looked uneasy as he wiped his sweating hands on his jeans. Pete led him to a punching bag hung from the backboard.

"I got you a bag set up," he said as he patted the stuffed canvas bag. "Here's some gloves." He handed the boy a scruffy pair of boxing gloves. "They'll help you with your coordination and your footwork." He draped a jump rope over the boy's arm. "The rope'll help you with your timing." Next he bounced a basketball back and forth between his right and left hands. "Alternate hands when you dribble. And don't look when you do. Let your hands feel where the ball is. And when you shoot," he said as he swished the ball through the hoop, "shoot with your fingertips. Get so used to having the ball in your hands that it feels like it's a part of you. Then you'll have the hands you need to make a good end."

"This mean you're gonna play me?"

"You start improvin'; I'll start playin' ya. But if ya keep fightin', I'm gonna keep ya on the bench."

Cheetah dropped the gloves and rope. "You think I'm just some wild horse, don't ya?"

"The wild ones you let go. It's the thoroughbreds you corral and put a saddle on."

Cheetah looked around the gym. "I feel like I'm bein' quarantined."

"Just on weeknights, to keep ya off the street and out of trouble. Get a good workout," he said as he walked away.

"Come on, Coach," he pleaded.

"See ya at ten."

After Pete left, Cheetah picked up the gloves and threw them against the wall. He sprang up the bleachers in bounding strides, watching from the window as Pete drove off, the tail lights of his Chevy shrinking into the night. He looked around the gym and, seeing no avenue of escape, paced back and forth on the bleachers, restive as a caged animal.

12

Pete left the parking lot and drove a couple of miles out of town to the Thompson place. Two lanterns glowed from the small farmhouse. One shone in the kitchen, revealing Gill's mother shelling black-eyed peas and his father gluing the wobbly leg of a wood chair. The other emitted a dim radius of light from a corner of the living room, its wick trimmed short so Gill could read without waking the other kids who were stretched out side-by-side on their pallets.

When Pete's Chevy pulled up, Gill met him at the door.

"Hello, Coach. Did my sister get word to ya?"

"That's why I stopped by."

Gill led him through the living room, where he tiptoed by the patchwork of sleeping kids and into the kitchen.

"How do, Coach Williams? We got some coffee left over from dinner. Wouldn't take no time to heat it up," offered Mrs. Thompson.

"No thank you; I'm fine. I was wanting to talk with you both about Gill. The boy's one of the finest lineman in the state. He's got a good chance at a scholarship if he continues to play like he did the other night and if he stays in school, keeps his grades up."

"I saw him play once," said Mr. Thompson. "Reminded me of a bunch of cows goadin' each other."

"What was it you said about 'scholarship'?" Mrs. Thompson broke in. "Exactly what is that?"

"If a boy agrees to play ball for a college, then the college agrees to put him through school."

"Ya mean, they sorta swap out?" asked Mr. Thompson.

"That's right," said Pete.

Mrs. Thompson reached her hand over to her husband's and squeezed it. "A Thompson in college. We never had no one on either of our sides go to college."

"We got too much ridin' on this crop; you know that. A lot of bills come due this month, and we can't afford to be givin' up our top hand."

"We could all double up, maybe get started a little sooner, quit a little later."

"Unless you got ways to bring the sun up earlier or make it go down later, I don't see how in the wide world we can do anymore than what we're doin'. We work from can to can't as it is." He could see her eyes pooling, but she held back the tears. "We all got to make sacrifices. Gill too." He turned to Pete. "Sorry I can't oblige ya, Coach Williams, but without Gill it'll take twice as long to bring in the crop. And we got a mortgage comin' due first of the month."

"I understand," said Pete.

He got up to leave, and Mrs. Thompson took a hanky from her apron to blot the corner of her eye. "I'll see ya to the door."

"Don't get up," he said, touching her shoulder. "I'll find my way out."

As he walked away, she buried her face in her hands, quietly releasing her tears. Pete paused and turned in the doorway.

"You a swappin' man, Mr. Thompson?"

"Depends what you're swappin'."

The next morning Pete wrote passes to get all the football players out of class. Billy delivered them. Each boy, in turn, gave the notes to their teachers. Cheetah and Hoot were the first ones out of class. As they walked down the hall, they saw Kathy coming toward them.

"How come you're out of class?" she asked.

"Got the day off," said Cheetah, a grin spreading across his face. "The whole day."

"Lucky."

"Yeah, see ya around."

As the two boys bounded down the steps, Hoot asked, "What kind of field trip do you think it is?"

All twenty-four boys along with Pete and the two managers were out in the Thompsons' field, walking down the rows of cotton, bending over to pull the white, little puffballs from their bolls.

"Field trip, my foot," Cheetah mumbled as he put a handful of cotton into a burlap sack. Fibber came up to him and began sniffing at that foot. "Go chase a rabbit. Go on, git!"

Mrs. Thompson brought water to Pete and to her husband, who was rubbing the small of his back. "Gill could maybe give the others a hand up when they get ready," she said, "teach 'em some things, maybe help them git into a school somewhere."

"Now don't go a plannin'. We ain't got the one in yet," he groused. But seeing the excitement in her eyes, he softened. He had almost forgotten the gleam that used to dance in those eyes so many years ago, so many children ago, so many hard times ago. He patted her hand and the beginnings of a smile cracked from his parched face. "But we'll work on it."

"I'll work on it too," said Pete. "I'll be on him to make

sure he plays good ball, but he's gonna need someone workin' with him to get his grades up and keep 'em up."

"Neither one of us can do that," she said. "We got no book learnin' past grade school."

"I don't know how you'll feel about it," said Pete, "but I thought of a way how to help him with that."

Most of the cotton crop got harvested that day, and what didn't, Mr. Thompson said he and the rest of the children could bring in by the end of the week.

The next day after practice Pete took Gill to live for the remainder of football season at the home of Herman and Winona Tucker. Herman was a banker and president of the Quarterback Club. Winona was a one-time school teacher and now part-time tutor.

When Gill put the few things he bundled up from home in the downstairs guest room, he ran his hands over the bedspread and mashed the mattress down a few times to test its springs. It was such a fine room that he had a hard time believing it was for him; even a harder time believing he had it all to himself.

He sat down to a dinner of roast beef, mashed potatoes and gravy, peas, a garden salad, milk, hot rolls and butter, and apple cobbler. He tried to be as polite as he could remember being taught, but they kept asking, "Won't you have some more?" And he didn't see why not, being that they were dividing all that food only three ways instead of the usual fifteen he was used to.

After dinner they showed him the bathroom and gave him a towel and washcloth so he could take a bath before going to bed. When they left, he looked around the bathroom in almost reverential awe. An indoor toilet. Tile everywhere. A mirror. A sink with hot and cold running water. A porcelain tub. Even a shower curtain and a store-bought bar of soap, fresh out of the wrapper.

He soaked in a tub of hot water for over an hour. He

just lay there, relaxing, letting the warm water soak away the dirt and soothe away his sore muscles. He took a deep breath and let his head go back and slip slowly under water, listening to the smallest of sounds echo off the tub. Underwater, he heard a knock and a muffled voice.

"You okay in there, Gill?" asked Mr. Tucker. Gill shot up out of the water and heard the knock clearly this time. "Anything wrong?"

"Oh, no, sir. Doin' great. Just finishin' up—"

"No hurry. We didn't hear anything, that's all, and—Well, no need to rush."

Gill dried off, combed his hair in front of the mirror, and put his old clothes back on. He toweled off the condensation on the mirror and wiped around the sink to blot off the water he had splashed over the counter. The slurpy vortex of draining water caught his attention, and he got on his knees to wipe away the strata of dirt that had been deposited around the tub. When he finished, he opened the door and walked into the kitchen to give Mrs. Tucker the dirty towel.

"That's some bathroom."

"Well, I'm . . . glad you like it," she said, somewhat at a loss for words. "Use it, eh, as often as, well, as you need to. Herman and I have our own."

"You mean you got another'n like that, inside?"

"It's upstairs."

"An inside, upstairs bathroom." Gill shook his head. "If that don't beat all. Well, I reckon I'll see you in the morning."

"Good-night."

"Oh," he said, turning, "do you need any help in the mornin'?"

"No."

"Ya sure? I'm used to workin' for my breakfast."

"You just work on your grades," she said, smiling, "I'll take care of breakfast."

Gill walked over to Mr. Tucker, who was reading the

paper in the living room. "Mighty nice place you have here, Mr. Tucker. You must be real proud."

"Thank you, Gill," he said. "We want you to make yourself at home while you're here."

"I mean to help out around the place with the chores and things like that."

"Now don't you worry about that. We want you putting all your effort into school."

"I'll work real hard, sir."

Later that night the Tuckers went to check on Gill. They inched open his door, and a wedge of light fell across his bed. He was asleep on top of the covers, still dressed in the clothes he wore when he arrived.

The breakfast table was draped in a bisque-colored table cloth with a vase of yellow roses carefully arranged in the center. The china was English, motifed with mauve clusters of hand-painted grapes, its leaves an almost translucent green, and its vines delicately encircling the perimeter of each plate. Breakfast consisted of a platter of scrambled eggs with grated cheddar cheese sprinkled on top, bacon, a plateful of toast with an assortment of jellies, a platter of sliced canteloupe, some generous slices of vine-ripened tomatoes, freshly squeezed orange juice, and a plump pitcher of milk.

After Mr. Tucker returned thanks, Gill looked up at both of them and said, "I never knew living could be this good."

Whenever the team scrimmaged, it left only two boys, besides the managers, on the sidelines: Willie D. and Cheetah.

After a few hard-fought downs, one of the boys got cleated and hobbled painfully off the field. Pete looked to the sidelines for a substitution. Both boys stood waiting and eager.

"Willie D., go in for Blake." The boy put on his helmet and went in to take the lineman's place.

Cheetah looked down at Fibber to catch the dog looking up at him. "What are *you* lookin' at?"

After the workout the boys started off for the long walk back to the school. Susie, Mary Ellen, and Kathy sat in a car around the corner, waiting for them as "Jersey Bounce" played over their radio.

"Quick, they're finished," said Kathy. Susie started the car and put it in gear when Mary Ellen ducked down.

"They're looking this way!" The other two girls slid down in their seats.

"Did they see us?" whispered Mary Ellen.

"I don't think so," whispered Susie. There was an anxious pause.

"Why are we whispering?" whispered Kathy, and they all started giggling.

"Back up and go around the block," said Mary Ellen.

Susie maneuvered the stick shift into reverse from her slumped position and accidentally honked the horn. The boys looked down the street at their car, but it appeared empty.

"Oops," said Susie.

"Swell."

"Try it again," said Kathy. Susie jiggled the stick into gear and backed up, only to run onto a curb and crumple a trash can.

"Oh, really swell," said Mary Ellen. The boys looked up again to see the car lurch forward and die. It lurched and died twice more before making a U-turn to circle the block.

With one arm casually draped over the steering wheel and her elbow sunning in the window, Susie nonchalantly pulled up beside the string of boys that were walking down the street.

"Hey, Susie," said Byron. "How about a ride?"

"Sure, hop in."

He got in the front seat, and a couple of other boys piled in the back, while several others sat on the hood and stood on the back bumper. She drove the car slowly down the street, trying to stretch out those brief, envious moments with the boys as long as possible. Pete's car passed them with Billy in the backseat. He spotted Kathy and looked through the rear window and waved, but she didn't see him.

One by one the boys straggled into the locker room. Billy and Hoot came carrying the equipment box. "Try to get 'em out by five-thirty," said Pete. "I need to shop around for a washing machine tonight."

They put the box down, and Billy got his paddle from the equipment cage. He slapped it flat against the wooden box and called out over the noise. "Listen up. Coach wants everyone out by five-thirty, so get in gear if ya don't wanna get busted."

Fifteen minutes later Billy again slapped his paddle against the equipment box. "Five-thirty. Everybody out."

As Billy swept through the locker room, the boys took flight like a flurry of dust before an angry broom. Except for Cheetah. He stood before the mirror in blue jeans and bare feet, taking his time as he buttoned his shirt.

"Clear out, Cheetah."

Cheetah continued buttoning his shirt. "Keep your shirt on, Button."

"Coach said five-thirty."

Cheetah pulled the comb from his back pocket and raked it leisurely through his hair. Billy then drew back his paddle and walloped him.

"Ouch! Why you little—" Cheetah shouted as he took off after him. Billy ran under a table and Cheetah vaulted over it in hot pursuit, chasing him into the equipment cage where Hoot was dressing a cut on Byron's arm. Billy ran between them, dropping his paddle as he did. Hoot and Byron caught Cheetah and held him at bay.

"Hey, hey, ease up, Cheetah, ease up!" hollered Hoot.

Cheetah ignored him and struggled to get at Billy, who

had taken refuge behind a trash can full of old equipment. "I told you if you ever did that again—"

"That's enough, Brown!" said Byron.

But Cheetah continued railing. "—Walk around here like a little Hitler, bossin' people around like you owned the place—"

Byron grabbed a handful of Cheetah's shirt. "I said, that's enough!" The two stood in each other's face. The only thing that averted a fight was the opening of the door to the coach's office. Pete came out and saw the four in the equipment cage, oblivious to the flaring tempers. "Time to go home, boys."

Cheetah turned to walk away, and his foot hit the wooden paddle. He reached down and picked it up, his eyes throwing daggers at Billy. He straightened up and hung the paddle on a hook, then walked away.

The next day in English class Byron was talking with the girl behind him when Billy skated into the room, barely beating the tardy bell. Byron looked over at him, smiling.

"Flirtin' with Kathy again?" Billy smiled back and raised his eyebrows. Byron looked past him, and Cheetah came into focus on the next row, sending Byron's smile in retreat.

In the gym that night the punching bag recoiled from a hard punch by Cheetah's right hand. He hit the bag again and again and again. Each time faster. Each time more forcefully. Sweat poured from his angry face. The fusillade of punches was exhausting him, but he kept up the rapid fire, relentlessly, ruthlessly, as he vented his anger on the canvas bag. He threw one final punch and then pushed the bag away.

Pete stood in a secondhand store that was getting ready to close, listening to the spin cycle of an old washing machine thump against its metal casing. He raised his voice so the owner could hear him. "Sounds awful loud."

"Good repairman could quiet her down. For the money,

you could afford him to completely rebuild it and you'd still come out ahead." He shut off the machine. "Way ahead."

"Do you deliver?"

"At that price?"

"No, I, eh, I guess not," said Pete self-consciously.

He trundled the washer home sideways in his trunk, lashed down by a snarl of bailing wire. On the way, he picked up Billy to help him unload and check over the used machine. They struggled to get it out of the trunk but finally managed to clunk it down onto the driveway.

"Careful," said Pete. "I want it to be a surprise." The unbalanced symmetry of the movers made carrying the washer awkward; Pete at six foot two, Billy at four feet even. "Easy now. Steady. Steady."

"Watch the step, Coach."

"Okay," he grunted, "up." Billy stood at the base of the steps, and Pete stood two rungs up.

"Wait a minute," said Billy.

"What?"

"Set her down." They strained to balance the washing machine on the steps, then both stood up to catch their breath. "Trade places." They held onto the precariously perched machine as they circled it. "Okay, now lift." Once they finally got it on the back porch, Pete wiped the sweat from his forehead and sighed. The back porch light went on. "Uh, oh, we been found out." Beth opened the door.

"Delivery for Mrs. Pete Williams," said Billy, smiling.

"Oh my gosh, a washer!"

"Now it's gonna need a little work, but Billy thought he could fix it."

"That's okay, here, let me get the door," said Beth. And they painstakingly inched it through the doorway into the kitchen.

At Cheetah's house the men scooted their chairs up to the table. On account of the game, his mother served supper early that night. A yellow pyramid of cornbread rose from a platter in the middle of the table. At the far end stood a steaming pot of stew. Next to Cheetah rested a bowl of fried okra, hot out of the oil. He reached over and popped a piece into his mouth. This raised an eyebrow from his mother but was not enough of an indiscretion to raise a word. The crispy morsel held within it a hot pocket of grease that he tried to cool by batting it about with his tongue.

"Return thanks for us, John Henry," said his mother.

As the men bowed their heads, he doused the burn with a drink of milk and hurriedly prayed: "We thank Thee for the bounty of which we are about to partake and for Thy mercies which are new every morning. Amen."

Cheetah's mother ladled out stew as each man relayed his plate to the end of the table. After Cheetah took a generous helping of okra, he passed it to his uncle. Clyde eyed his plate and commented, "Don't want to be fillin' up too much before the game."

"Yeah," Cheetah replied sarcastically.

"You gonna pway football tonight, huh, John Henwy?" asked Sydney. "I go watch you?"

"Not tonight," said Cheetah through a mouthful of cornbread and downed half his glass of milk in one swallow.

"I be good, I pwomise. Let me watch you pway. Pwease, I come along. I won't bodder nobody."

"You talk too much at the table, Sydney." Cheetah scraped his chair back and looked at his mother. "May I be excused?"

That night as Nadine washed dishes the old men gathered in their rocking chairs around the radio on the windowsill on the front porch. The announcer's voice grew with excitement the closer McKinney came to the goal line: "McKinney's on the Jesuit eight-yard line. Third and inches.

Simms flanked wide to the right. Long count. Jeffers takes the snap, fakes to Jones up the middle, and bootlegs around right end! He's in for the score! Touchdown!"

A cheer arose from the men on the porch. The game was like a tonic, and with each quarter they could feel their youth returning to them.

By the time Cheetah arrived home from the victory, it was late and all the men had gone to bed; all except Uncle Clyde, who was leisurely puffing away.

"Evenin', John Henry."

"Evenin', Uncle Clyde. Up kinda late, aren't we?"

"We are," he said and took a long pull on his pipe.

Cheetah reached for the handle on the screen door and stopped. "You're not in trouble with Ma again, are you?"

"Nope."

He opened the screen and hesitated again. "*I'm* not in trouble with Ma again, am I?"

"Don't think so." The boy looked relieved. "Dropped yer sock there, Son." Cheetah bent down to pick it up. "Good game tonight. Two in a row; longest win streak we've had around these parts in some time."

Cheetah turned to air his frustration. "He hadn't played me one down, Uncle Clyde. Not one. It's like he, it's like— ah, forget it." And he went inside.

Cheetah moped away the weekend and plodded listlessly through Monday's workout. Once again he was sentenced to the sidelines as the squads paired off to work on some new offensive plays. He chewed on a dried stalk of grass, wondering what in the world he was doing there, thinking he didn't need this, that he had better things to do with his afternoons.

He watched for a few plays, then took a few inconspicuous steps back and pouted off down the street, unnoticed. The farther he got from the practice field the bolder he got in voicing his complaints. By the time he reached the locker room he didn't care who heard him.

"—sick o' tryin' to please that man, sick and tired," he argued with himself as he threw his helmet into the equipment cage. The noise caught the attention of Billy, who was repairing the washing machine.

"What are ya doin' in so early?"

"I'm hangin' it up; I quit."

"You what?"

Cheetah started pulling the jersey over his head. "I'm wastin' my time out there."

The jersey stuck on his shoulder pads, and Billy came over to help. "I work my tail off in practice—" Billy yanked at the jersey, and it finally came off. "—sweatin' through the drills, pukin' my guts out after windspints—" Cheetah sat down on the bench, untying the string on his shoulder pads. "—and he don't so much as look my way on the sidelines."

"You think you *should* be playin'?" Cheetah was silent. "You think all the other boys just suited up and became starters overnight? Wilemon, Thompson, Freight Train? It took time. They all had to pay their dues." Cheetah continued shedding his uniform. "Last year when Highland Park was kickin' 'em all over the field, it was *their* faces gettin' smashed, *their* backs that had the cleat marks." Billy got up to retrieve Cheetah's helmet and handed it to him.

"I'll never get a chance to pay a dime's worth o' dues 'cause he's never gonna play me. I just wanna get in a game and prove myself, that's all."

Billy looked at him and didn't respond.

"What?"

Billy just shook his head.

"Say it."

But Billy wouldn't.

"Go ahead. Ya got somethin' to say, say it."

Billy looked Cheetah straight in the eye without so much

as a blink coming between them. "I'd give anything just to be able to put on a McKinney uniform. Wouldn't matter if I ever played a down; just to be able to suit up with the rest of the team and stand on the sidelines . . . that'd be enough." Billy bent down to pick up Cheetah's jersey. "I'll check your equipment if that's what you want. But you're makin' a mistake."

That night Cheetah sulked through dinner and excused himself to his room. He shut the door and plopped onto his bed, putting his hands behind his head on the pillow. He lay there, staring at the ceiling. The moonlight spilled through the open window and softly washed the room. There was a gentle knock on his door.

"It's open."

His mother opened the door. "You okay, Son?"

"Uh huh."

"You're not crossways with the Jeffers boy again, are ya?"

"It's not that."

"Then what?"

"Nuthin'."

She came into the room and sat on the end of his bed and started rubbing his ankle.

"Your ankles still bother ya?"

"Sometimes."

"They botherin' ya now?"

"A little."

She continued rubbing, humming the tune to "Rock of Ages," then softly sang:

> . . . *Let me hide myself in Thee.*
> *Let the water and the blood*
> *From Thy riven side which flowed*
> *Be of sin the double cure*
> *Cleanse me from its guilt and power.*

Cheetah interrupted her before she could start the second verse. "I'm thinkin' 'bout quittin' football." The silence in the room seemed to gather weight and almost take on human dimensions the longer it continued.

"Why?"

"Things just aren't workin' out."

She stood up and walked to the window. "Thirteen years ago things weren't workin' out for your father. Job wasn't workin' out. Marriage wasn't. Fatherhood. Woke up one mornin' an' wanted out. Up an' quit, just like that." She walked over to the door, weary from the years of carrying the weight of a household on her shoulders. She stopped in the doorway. "I know it hadn't been easy for ya." She paused. "Hadn't been easy for me either." And she quietly shut the door behind her.

13

The next day the players had suited up in their game uniforms for the team picture and were horsing around a little while the photographer adjusted his tripod. Pete was on one end wearing a T-shirt with a whistle draped around his neck. Next to him stood Ted Murphy. The managers were on the other side; Hoot, with his hands in his back pockets, Billy bent down on one knee.

Absent from the three rows of emerging manhood was Cheetah. The photographer looked at them. "Need to squeeze in a little." They squinched together, and the photographer framed them through his lens. "Bunch-in a little more. Okay, everybody real still."

"Wait!" Billy called out as he saw Cheetah running up the street, pulling his jersey over his head.

"Sorry I'm late," he said as he passed Pete to take his place on the end of the row next to Billy.

The photographer squinted through his camera and snapped the shutter. The picture was later prominently displayed in Woolworth's window between a team roster and a schedule of upcoming games. The store owner placed a sign over the display: THIS YEAR'S McKINNEY LIONS.

In spite of the fact that Cheetah's stint in the gym kept him off the streets on weeknights, there were still weekends.

And there were still Mill District kids wanting to prove themselves. Fighting Cheetah was kind of a rite of passage for them. Just to be able to say they challenged him or went five minutes with him or landed a punch on him, that meant something, something they could brag about among themselves. Whenever Pete found out about it, though, he sentenced the boy to another week on the bench, parole coming on the basis of good behavior or it wasn't coming at all.

During the weeks ahead, Cheetah sat on that bench, where week after week he watched the team steadily improve. He watched Gill grow into his leadership role as team captain. He watched Freight Train establish himself as a power runner with breakaway speed. He watched Byron develop as a passer.

The Saturday paper that was passed around the barber shop chronicled the improvement: *Lions Devour Bonham 32–0. Thompson Leads Lions with 12 Unassisted Tackles. McKinney Outlasts Gainsville 13–6. Jones Scores Winning Touchdown. Lions Shut Out Arlington 21–0. Jeffers Passes for Three TDs. McKinney Edges Sulphur Springs 13–6. Defensive Teamwork Saves Game.*

The McKinney Lions were winning again. They won because, more than anything else, they wanted to please Coach. They wanted to please him because he believed in them, whether anyone else did or not, and somehow that made believing in themselves a little easier. They wanted to please him because of the way he smiled as he put his arm around their shoulder, asking how things were going at home or in the classroom. They wanted to please him because they knew he would do anything in the world to help them with whatever it was they needed help with. That's why they worked so hard. That's why they endured so much. And that's why they won.

Winning on Friday nights meant McKinney football was news again. Big news. Sales for the Saturday edition of the

Gazette soared higher with every Friday-night win. And with every win the boys grew more confident, more determined, more convinced that they could hold their own with Highland Park. As they worked their Saturday jobs, stacking sacks of cement or unloading boxes of canned goods, "Beat Highland Park" was exhaled with every heave. It became the obsession that arched over every ambition of their young lives. For those twenty-six boys there was no horizon beyond Dallas, no time beyond November.

It was November now, and the hangover heat from summer was gone. Shirtsleeves in the stands turned to sweaters. Cheetah continued to work hard both on the field and at the gym. He was up to five hundred jumps with the rope without a miss. His timing was coming along, as was his coordination. He was moving his feet better, bobbing and weaving. His jabs were sharper, more precise; his punches, more powerful. He was dribbling the basketball with either hand now, developing a feather touch, shooting from the top of the key and knocking the bottom out of the bucket. In practice his moves were quicker; he was diving for the ball more, concentrating better, making fingertip catches.

Billy worked with him after practice, running him through agility drills, timing him with a stopwatch as he ran windsprints. Everyone was beginning to notice the change.

But one thing didn't change. He still couldn't pass up a chance to pop a smart aleck in the mouth or to even out the odds when one of his buddies was being ganged-up on. He was never one to back down from a fight. And though he stopped looking for fights, they continued looking for him.

"How's the Brown boy doing?" asked Beth as she dished out a slithery mound of spaghetti onto Pete's plate.

"He's comin' along. I think he could start for us if ever he could go a week without fightin'."

Pete lifted the strands with his fork and probed around.

"What are you looking for?"

"Thought there might be a meatball hiding in there somewhere."

"Havta wait till the first of the month for meatballs." Beth sat down and filled her plate. "Lynell called. Wanted to introduce me around at their monthly Garden Club meeting."

"That's great."

"I told her I'd talk it over with you and call her back."

"What's to talk about?"

"I dunno. I mean, I won't know anybody there, except Lynell."

He finished tying his shoes and stood up. "They're just people, hon. Good, down-home type of people."

"I'm not like you. I can't . . . It's harder for me, that's all."

He looked down at his watch. "Gotta go." And he took one last bite of spaghetti.

"Do you have to?"

"I'm speaking at the Quarterback Club, and then I've got to swing by the gym and take John Henry home."

She saw him to the door, where he kissed her good-bye, then watched him get into the old gray Chevy and back it out of the dirt driveway.

"'Night, hon," he said.

"Good-night."

Bathed in yellow porch light, she waved to him. After he drove off, she stood in the doorway, feeling the faint breeze whisper to her of home. She thought about the cool, tree-lined streets of the homey, Chicago suburb she left behind. She left behind her neighborhood, her family, everything that was safe and familiar and a part of her. She left them behind for a man who took her to Texas and who, with the wand of one expedient decision, waved it and turned her into a coach's wife; turned a shy little girl into a coach's wife who was expected to go places and do things and make conversation with people she didn't even know. She thought about the familiar sidewalks back home that she used to bike down with such carefree, windblown ease as a child. It dawned on her she might never see those sidewalks again. And as she stood framed in that doorway, a solitary tear slid down her cheek.

In the gym that night Cheetah was attacking the canvas punching bag, tributaries of sweat channeling down his face. He stopped when he heard a key jiggling the lock to the door. It opened to reveal Pete. "Ten o'clock, hoss. Ready to go home?"

"Just about." Cheetah hit the bag a few times more. Pete came over to steady it.

After a vigorous volley of punches, he started unlacing his gloves. "Pretty good," said Pete.

"Good enough to play?"

"Had any fights lately?"

"Been over a week now. Look, I know I don't deserve to start. I just wanna chance to prove myself, that's all."

"Keep your gloves on." Pete helped him with the laces. "Show me what you got." Pete backed away from him, just out of the boy's reach. "Don't hold back."

"I don't want to hurt ya," Cheetah said, smiling. Pete lifted his hands to square off against the boy. The smile suddenly retreated from Cheetah's face as did his jocular mood. "'Course, I don't want you hurtin' me either."

"Come on; show me."

Cheetah reluctantly raised his gloves. Pete took a swipe at the boy and slapped his cheek.

Momentarily stunned, Cheetah raised his gloves again, this time balling them into fists. He took a couple of tentative jabs, which Pete slapped down.

Pete feinted left, right, then struck another palm against Cheetah's face. This time a little blood seeped from one of his nostrils. He wiped it away with the back of his glove and looked at it. He started to move now, working his feet, bobbing his head and shoulders. He drew in his guard and jabbed sharply. Pete threw a right, and Cheetah blocked it. He threw a left. Again, he countered it. Pete made another advance, and Cheetah rammed a glove through an opening, connecting with his face. Pete staggered back and checked his jaw, moving it back and forth.

"You okay, Coach?" Cheetah lowered his gloves and stepped toward him.

Pete struck like a coiled snake, then came at him, slapping Cheetah back, and back, and back some more, until at last the boy ducked and maneuvered to Pete's back side. When Pete turned, he was met with a right hook that hit him with the force of a wrecking ball. Cheetah moved into him with a vengeance, pummeling him with body punches to his sides and stomach. Pete tried to fend him off, but the boy kept hitting him, faster and harder. Finally Pete wrapped his arms around the fury to restrain the whirlwind of punches.

"Enough. Enough!" Cheetah struggled to free himself, but Pete squeezed until he subdued him. "That's the bell; it's over. It's over."

As the tension drained from the taut, catlike sinews of Cheetah's body, Pete released his hold. Cheetah backed away and started pulling at the laces in his gloves with his teeth. Pete reached for one of the gloves. The boy resisted at first, but Pete pulled it toward him and started undoing the laces.

"When you're in the ring, you want to channel that anger through your fist," Pete said. "Outside the ring, you want to channel it somewhere else; have it work *for* ya rather than against ya."

Pete took a handkerchief from his pocket and staunched the trickle of blood that drained from Cheetah's nose. He ran his fingers down the bridge of that nose, checking to see if it was broken. "That hurt?"

"A little."

"Lay down and put your head back."

Cheetah stretched out on a bleacher and put the handkerchief over his nose. "Where'd ya learn to fight like that?" the boy asked.

"Neighborhood I grew up in was all older kids, always pickin' on me. Used to come home cryin' so much that one day Papa grabbed me, said I ever come in cryin' again, he'd give me a whippin' on top of it. Then he showed me some things about defendin' myself, how to keep my guard up, duck a punch. Before long I could take up for myself pretty good."

Pete continued reminiscing as they walked to the parking lot. Cheetah hung on every word. "I remember how when we kids would step out of line, Mama wouldn't raise her voice, she'd just say, 'I'll have to tell Papa when he gets home.' And we'd go on playin', like nuthin' happened—until Papa got home. After supper he'd read at the table from the big, family Bible. When he finished, he'd look over his five-and-dime glasses and say, 'Mama, is there anything I need to know?' And she'd tell him, calmly, 'Petie'—that's what they used to call me—'Petie ran off without doin' his chores,' or 'Petie sassed me.' And you could see his jaws tighten, his nostrils gettin' stiff. He'd fold up his reading glasses, close the Book, and say, 'Come on, Son.' And we'd go to the woodshed for a switchin'."

The conversation continued as Pete drove Cheetah home. "He still livin'?"

"Died shortly after I got out of the army. One of my fondest memories was seein' him walkin' home from work at the end of each day, his coveralls, that ol' black lunch pail of his. And somehow, somehow ya just knew that however rough things got, they'd work out . . . 'cause Papa was there." He sighed as he pulled up in front of Cheetah's house. "I'd give anything to see him walkin' down that street again, in those coveralls, that lunch pail bobbin' by his side."

"Least ya got some good memories. Not the same as havin' him here, but it's somethin', ya know. Mine left when I was three, so there's not much to look back on."

"Seen him since?"

Cheetah shook his head.

"A letter, anything?"

"Nope. Don't even know if he's alive. I wonder sometimes where he is, what he's doin', what he looks like now after all these years. Sometimes at night I stare at the ceilin', wonderin' if he ever wonders about me like that. . . . 'Course, I 'spect it was me the reason he left in the first place."

"Why do you say that?"

"I dunno; just always figured it was."

"What would you do if he came back?"

"If he came back?" Cheetah asked with a laugh. "Prob'ly bust him upside the head, you know me."

"And then?"

"Then I'd ask him why he walked out of our lives, puttin' all that load on Mama. And then, then I'd ask him to come home . . . so we could be a family, have someone to ride herd on me, maybe take me huntin' or fishin' now and then, or whatever fathers do now and then with their sons."

Pete eased his car to a stop in front of the boy's house, then moved his jaw back and forth with his hand. "Way to channel that anger."

"Sorry about that."

"Don't be. It was a good punch."

"Thanks for the ride." Cheetah opened the door and got out.

"Sure."

He walked a step, then turned. "Good-night, Coach. Enjoyed hearin' 'bout yer dad."

"Night, Son."

14

It was Saturday night, a week before the homecoming game with Denton, as a crowd stood in line for tickets to see *The Best Years of Our Lives* at the Ritz Theater.

"Who ya takin' to homecoming?" Hoot asked Byron.

"Susie, I think. How 'bout you?"

"Thought about askin' Loretta."

"You takin' anybody, Billy?" Hoot asked.

"I dunno."

"What about Kathy?"

"I thought about it."

"She's inside; why don't ya ask her?"

Billy looked in the lobby to see Kathy and Mary Ellen buying popcorn. "I'll call her tomorrow."

The boys settled in the center section with the girls in the rows in front of them. They watched as the three soldiers on the screen made their way home after the war: Fredric March, an alcoholic sergeant, returning to his wife, his children, and his job at the bank; Dana Andrews, an air force captain, to his new bride and a job as a soda jerk; and Harold Russell, a sailor who had lost both hands in battle, to his parents, his high school sweetheart, and to the stares of the neighborhood children. It was an Academy-Award-winning performance for Russell, but for Billy it was pure agony to watch the handicapped man looming larger than life on the big screen.

The next day while Billy was working on Beth's washing machine, his stubby fingers felt as awkward as the hooks on Harold Russell's hands. He fumbled with a pair of pliers in the cramped inner workings of the machine.

"I really appreciate your stopping by. Pete isn't real mechanical."

"Glad I could help." He strained to tighten the belt to the motor. "There, that ought to do it." He got up and switched on the machine for a second, then switched it off again.

"Sounds great, and just in time; I needed to wash a dress for the Garden Club meeting tomorrow. They want me to give a little talk on how Pete and I met, when we got married, what brought us to McKinney, stuff like that."

"That's quite an honor."

"I'm scared to death. Silly, isn't it, grown woman being afraid like that?"

"Everybody's got things they're afraid of, Mrs. Williams, just different things with different people, that's all."

"I've been that way since I was a little girl."

"When I was little and lyin' in bed at night, I used to see the bogeyman in my closet. And I just knew he was waitin' till I was asleep so he could make his move and get me. Talk about scared. I couldn't even get out of bed or call for someone to turn on the light. But ya know what, Mrs. Williams? When I stared down that bogeyman, he turned out to be a coat hangin' in the closet. That's all, just a coat."

"Yeah, but you're such an outgoing person. The family I came from, it wasn't—"

"Mrs. Williams, I gotta stare down things all the time. Every day I get dressed and look in the mirror I—" A sudden stir of emotion began to unsettle him.

Beth put her hand on his shoulder and tried to console him. "Your parents have a lot to be proud of, Billy, you know that?"

"My parents gave me up for adoption; another one of those things I havta stare down. My grandparents are the ones ended up adoptin' me." Billy tried to squeeze out a smile. "Way I look at it, least they kept me in the family."

The next day Beth spent the morning getting ready for the Garden Club meeting. It was being held at the Jeffers' house, which made her feel more comfortable about going, and it was being hosted by Lynell Jeffers, which made her feel even more comfortable. Lynell was all that was good about the Old South: genteel, hospitable, unhurried . . . a person you could sip lemonade with on a porch swing, the soothing lilt of her voice passing by you like a river.

But still, there would be people there she didn't know, people who were established in the community, women with new clothes and nice homes, women who didn't have to sweat the end of the month and could cook decent meals for their husbands, women who could flit around from one topic of conversation to another, women who had something that she didn't—a college education.

Pete came by and picked her up at a quarter till ten. Beth was in front of the mirror, adjusting her dress, then taking the tip of a hanky and wiping away a little smudge of lipstick.

"You look great," said Pete as he came up behind her and kissed her on the neck.

"I look awful."

"Come on, are you kidding? You look terrific."

"You really think so?" She checked the mirror for a second opinion.

Pete put his arms around her waist and turned her around. "It'll be okay, Beth. Just relax and be yourself."

By the time they arrived at the Jeffers' house it was

10:00 A.M. Hundred-year-old live oak trees spread their branches over the yard in leafy parasols of shade. The white frame house was a neatly kept one-story with dormer windows on the roof and a white picket fence around the yard.

"I'll walk you," offered Pete.

"Thanks."

They got out of the car and walked around to the backyard where folding chairs were arranged in chatty little circles of fives and sixes, women with plates of refreshments on their laps, effervescing with small-town talk. Beth looked out over the yard and imagined it to be one big closet and all the women, just so many coats, hanging there; *just coats,* she told herself, *nothing to be afraid of.*

"Beth," said Lynell as she came and hugged her. "Good to see you, child; so glad you could come." She extended her hand to Pete. "And Coach Williams, what a delight. Won't you join us?"

"Thank you, but I need to get back to school."

Pete kissed Beth on her ear and whispered, "You'll do fine."

"Everyone's real excited to meet you, don't ya know."

"Really?" asked Beth.

"Sure enough. I declare, we haven't had a turnout like this since the ex-governor's wife came to dedicate that bust of her husband in the county courthouse."

Pete left Beth with Lynell, her arm wrapped securely around Beth's waist, and the host took her around to meet the other women. They were spread out like a counterpane, a pattern of circles spaced evenly over the backyard.

"Jolene, Mary Elizabeth, I'd like yawl to meet a friend of mine, Beth Williams."

"So you're the coach's wife," said Jolene, extending her hand. "Pleased to meet you."

And somehow, with Lynell's arm around her waist and

being introduced as her friend, Beth began to feel she had found a place in the community, a place where she fit.

Before going back to the high school Pete drove down Tennessee Street and pulled into Willard Kincaid's driveway. He rapped on the door, and Mrs. Kincaid welcomed him in. As she went to get her husband, Pete looked around the meticulously kept room. His eyes stopped on the mantle, where picture frames chronicled three generations of Kincaids that went back to the Civil War. Pictures of stern men and sterner women posed stiffly in their Sunday best, their flinty faces having been chipped against the steel of a hard life.

His eyes followed the line of pictures and came to four Confederate soldiers; brothers, from the looks of their faces. Proudly posed in dress gray. Sabers sheathed at their sides. Eyes agleam in anticipation of war.

The next picture showed only one of those brothers. A crutch stood to his side where once was a saber; a stump, where once was a leg. His eyes were sunken, as if his very soul had been sucked out of him, leaving behind only a shriveled shell of the man he once was.

"M'grandfather," Kincaid said, looking over Pete's shoulder. "War cost him a leg, three brothers, and his farm. Burned to the ground in Sherman's march to the sea. Sounds noble, don't it? His *march* to the sea. Sixty-two thousand men burnin', lootin', destroyin' everythin' they couldn't cart off or eat. Shootin' livestock for sport, terrorizin' women and children while their men were off fightin'. Only thing left standin' when m'grandfather came home was the chimney."

"I saw a lot of terrible things happen in war, to both sides."

"Sherman's march wasn't war; it was rape."

"But it's over now."

"For the North it's over; they won. But for us, we're still sufferin' for it. M'folks came to Texas to get a fresh start." He paused as his fingers touched the frame of their wedding picture. "How can you ever start fresh with memories like that houndin' ya wherever ya go?"

"I'm sorry about what happened to your family."

"Yes, well, I 'spect ya didn't come to swap war stories."

"No. I came to ask one more time about the equipment. The boys've worked really hard, come a long way. It'd give 'em a big boost to play the homecoming game with new uniforms."

"District finances aren't any better than the last time we talked. Can't squeeze blood out of a turnip."

"Can't blame me for tryin'," Pete said.

"No, I can't."

"Well, thanks for hearin' me out, anyway." He took a piece of paper out of his shirt pocket and handed it to him. Kincaid looked at the paper as if to decipher an explanation. "The uniform sizes. In case there's a windfall in the budget somewhere down the road."

Kincaid smiled and as Pete opened the door, he remarked, "Doin' a good job—" He smiled. "—for a Yankee."

It was the night of the homecoming game, and Uncle Clyde was laying on the horn to his jalopy. "Come on; we're gonna be late!"

"Keep your shirt on," said one of the men.

Clyde honked again. "Yawl keep dilly-dallyin' around and there won't be any seats left."

By the time they arrived at Newsome Stadium it was full. People had come from miles around, people who hadn't been to a McKinney game in years. They had come from every corner of the county, from town, from off the farm, and from Highland Park, scouting to see if this team was for real or if the scores in the papers had just been typographical errors. That night the scouts from Dallas found out the

McKinney Lions were for real. At the end of the first half they led an impressive Denton team 10–0.

Midway into the third quarter, however, the tide began to change. Denton scored, and, in the process, dislocated the shoulder of McKinney's left end. The boy came to the sidelines, wincing and cradling his arm. Pete ran an indecisive hand through his hair and looked down the bench where thirteen boys sat hungry to taste action. Cheetah was among those boys, looking like a junkyard dog, sitting on eager haunches, salivating for the least little bone to be thrown his way. His helmet was in hand, ready to go.

"Nelson." That's all Pete had to say, and the second string end was off and running onto the field. Cheetah's spirit suddenly deflated, the breath he had held so expectantly exhaled now in dejection.

It was 10–6 going into the fourth quarter when Nelson turned an ankle. He hopped off the field, and Pete again looked down the bench. The second string right end put on his helmet.

"Riley, go in for—" But he paused as he noticed Cheetah's helmet slip from his fingers to the grass beneath the bench. "No, wait. John Henry, take Nelson's place."

Cheetah shot off the bench and ran onto the field. Pete whistled. "Your helmet." Cheetah felt around on his head and sprinted back toward the sidelines, where Pete handed him his headgear.

Uncle Clyde stood up and squinted. "I think that's your boy, Nadine."

"That's him, all right," she said. "I can tell by the way he runs."

Cheetah took his place in the huddle, and Byron asked him, "Did Coach send in a play?"

Cheetah hesitated.

"Did he or didn't he?" asked Byron.

All eyes were on Cheetah. He nodded.

"Well?" asked Byron.

"Fake to the fullback . . . and, and drop back to pass . . . and . . ."

"Come on," Byron said impatiently.

"Fake to the right end comin' over the middle, and . . . and hit me goin' long. I'll be runnin' a post pattern."

The huddle was skeptical, and all eyes turned to Byron. "Okay. You heard him. On one."

They clapped and broke huddle. Each player got into position. Cheetah bit a nail before settling into his stance. He eyed the goalpost thirty yards away.

"Hut one!" The lines collided. Byron faked to the fullback, pumped to the end going over the middle, which drew in the defensive backs. He looked downfield. Cheetah had a man covering him, but he gave a head-and-shoulder fake, and cut toward the goalpost. Cheetah looked over his shoulder. The ball was already on its downward trajectory. He dived for it. His fingers touched the ball. He pulled it to his chest and fell with it into the end zone.

"Touchdown, McKinney!" echoed the antiquated public address system. The band roused to their feet with the fight song blaring from their horns and pounding from their drums. As Cheetah got up, his teammates swamped him. In the stands his mother, Uncle Clyde, and the elderly pensioners were on their feet, cheering wildly.

By the time the final gun sounded, the Lions ended up on top, 19–6. The McKinney players went wild on the field, not so much celebrating the victory as they were the fact that they would be playing Highland Park for the district championship.

The celebratory mood accompanied them into the locker room, where they quickly showered and dressed for the dance. Everyone had left except Billy and Hoot and a few others who were crowding the mirror, trying to get their ties tied right. Billy put on his slacks and shoes before he dashed a little hair tonic into his palm. He worked it into his hair, running a comb through it, careful to make sure it was all in place. After he put on his shirt and tie, he stood alone in front of that mirror, blotting the perspiration from his face. He danced a little jitterbug and spoke to the mirror.

"Snow White, here I come!"

15

When Billy entered the gym, the dance was in full swing with a small orchestra made up of band members playing "A String of Pearls." He waved to Gill, who was standing by himself with a plate full of finger sandwiches, and to a few girls that waved to him. The gym was decorated with streamers of gold-and-blue crepe paper, multicolored balloons, and butcher-paper banners painted by the yell leaders: *McKinney High Forever . . . Homecoming . . . 1946—The Year of the Lion . . . Welcome Back, Graduates.*

Billy shuttled his way through the intricate weave of couples to the refreshment table where several boys formed a wall of suits around the punch bowl.

The superintendent and a handful of teachers were sprinkled around the gym as chaperones. Among them was Elaine Caulfield.

Pete brought Beth over to meet her. "Miss Caulfield, I'd like ya to meet my wife Beth."

"Pleased to meet you, Beth," she said as she extended her hand.

"I've heard so much about you," said Beth and shook her hand.

"I don't doubt that," she said, looking over at Pete.

"It was good, I mean, what *I* heard, anyway. I mean—" Pete rubbed his hand reassuringly over her back. "What I heard was all good," she said more calmly, "and it came from a very reliable source."

"I daresay," Miss Caulfield said, smiling.

"Can I get you ladies some punch?"

"I'd love some, thank you," said the teacher.

Beth stood next to the prim and proper woman, and all of the sudden she felt like the kid who had to stay after school and found herself alone in terrifying proximity to her classroom teacher.

"I can't imagine an attractive and intelligent woman like yourself not being married," Beth said, just wanting to make conversation.

"Well, when I was young, I told myself I was just particular, waiting for the worthy suitor. Looking back, I think it was the suitor who was the particular one."

"I didn't mean it like—"

"At the time I thought my love for learning and teaching was enough, that I didn't need anything else, or anybody else. Now, I have my books, a fastidious cat, an occasional letter from a retrospectively grateful student, and, I guess, a certain professional fulfillment."

"But you have a college education, a degree. I mean, a teacher, that's, that's something important you're doing with your life."

She looked up to see the Pete maneuvering his way through the jostling crowd. "Yes, I suppose you're right." She looked at Beth and smiled. "But I'd trade it all for someone who would walk across a crowded gym floor to bring me punch."

Pete came back with three cups, half filled. He extended them apologetically. "'Fraid I spilled a little on the way over."

Beth took her cup and hooked her arm in his. "Thank you, hon." She smiled at him, looking playfully into his eyes.

"What?" he asked, as if some secret had surreptitiously

traded hands. He looked at Miss Caulfield. "Did I miss somethin'?"

Miss Caulfield patted him on the arm. "Thank you for the punch."

The band played "Paper Doll" as Byron and two other football players stepped up to the microphone and harmonized to the popular Mills Brothers' song.

Billy's feet were tapping to the music as his eyes searched the gym for Kathy. They looked for her on the dance floor, at the punch bowl, and among the amorous shadows of the gym's poorly lit corners, but she was nowhere to be found. Billy felt a tap on his shoulder. He turned, and there she was, her satin and chiffon formal softly catching the light, the pink of her dress taking on an opalescent quality.

"Wow! You look beautiful."

"Oh, you're so sweet, Billy. Why can't all the boys be like you."

The band started playing "On the Atcheson, Topeka, and the Sante Fe."

"Wanna dance?" Billy asked.

"Sure," she said, and they both jitterbugged to the middle of the floor. Then several of the couples began to link up in a human train, picking up passengers as they chugged a circuitous route through the gym.

When the song was over, she bent down and kissed him on the cheek. "Save me another dance."

"Okay."

"Promise?"

"Cross my heart."

The band started playing "Twilight Time," and she was whisked away by her good-looking date who swept her into his arms and onto the dance floor. Billy retreated to the refreshment table.

"Have some of these sandwiches, Billy. The pimento

cheese is the best, if you ask me," said Gill. "'Course it takes four or five of 'em to make a regular sandwich."

He stood looking around the dance floor for Kathy, picking away at a plate of sandwiches and cookies when Fibber sauntered through the gym door. He nosed around to find out what all the commotion was about, looking for a little attention, expecting a handout or two to fall his way. When he spotted Billy, he wiggled his stubby little tail and trotted across the gym, parting dancers.

"What are you doin' here?" Billy said under his breath. "Come here." The dog stopped. "Come here, I said." Billy picked him up and carried him to an exit. "You can't be here." He dropped the dog outside the gym. "Now go home." But Fibber just stood there looking at him. "Go on, git." The dog backed up a few steps. Billy picked up a rock and hit him. "Go on, ya little mutt." And the dog turned tail for home.

After the music stopped, the dance floor thinned, some of the dancers going outside for some fresh air, some walking hand-in-hand to the refreshment table. It was there that Miss Caulfield caught a glimpse of Ted Murphy. Seeing him in a coat and tie instead of his usual work clothes caused her to look at him in a suddenly different light, a softer light, a light that hid the fact that he never finished high school.

Standing in line, he saw her too and waved. Somewhat self-consciously, she waved back, then turned her head. The music started again, and the gym floor soon became a crush of high-school kids losing themselves in the moment.

Cheetah walked by and noticed Miss Caulfield standing alone and thought it wouldn't do his grades any harm if he happened to let a compliment slip out and fall her way.

"Evenin', Miss Caulfield."

"Hello, John Henry. Heard you were quite the star tonight."

"I have to confess, I did shine a little." He took a step back. "I also have to confess . . . the way you look in that dress, if I was forty years older, I'd be mighty tempted to ask you for a dance."

Miss Caulfield wrinkled her brow.

"Did I say forty? I meant thirty." He could sense his grades dropping. "Or somewheres between twenty and thirty." Her eyes softened. "Closer to twenty, actually." Which brought a smile to her face, and he felt hopeful that when it came time to averaging his grades, this moment would factor in favorably. But still, he didn't want to press it. "Well, I'd like to stay and talk, but, uh, the punch, my date, she's waitin' for it."

"You may be excused, John Henry."

"Thank you, Miss Caulfield."

The next time Miss Caulfield looked up, she saw Ted Murphy, two cups of punch in his hands, carefully picking his way through the crowded dance floor.

"Thought you might like some punch, Miss Caulfield."

"Elaine. Please." She took the cup from his hand. "Thank you—"

"Ted," he interrupted and then smiled.

"Ted."

Toward the end of the evening the dance floor started thinning out, some of the couples wanting to stop off at the Rockpit and park a while before the evening was over. But Billy kept waiting for one more dance with Kathy. He went over to Byron and requested the song "Candy." As Byron and the other two members of the trio sang, Billy saw her. He started to get her attention but backed off when he saw her date whisper in her ear and kiss her neck. She nodded. Her date put his arm around her shoulder, and they both walked out of the gym.

Billy sat down in a chair while the last song of the evening was played. "Stardust."

"Need a ride?" asked Beth.

"What? Nah, I'll walk; it's not that far."

"It's on our way," said Pete.

They finally talked him into coming, and he sat enveloped in the darkness of the backseat as they drove down the lamp-lit streets to his house.

"How did you like the dance?" asked Beth.

"Okay."

"Just okay?"

"Uh huh."

"Always this excited after a dance?" joked Pete. But no answer came from the backseat.

"Something wrong, Billy?" Beth asked. "You can tell us."

He looked out the window as he spoke. "I may get a dance with Snow White, but when the music's over, she'll be drivin' home with the prince—not the dwarf."

The car came to a stop in front of his house. "Snow Whites and handsome princes don't live in McKinney, Billy. Only in picture shows, in a world of make believe."

Billy got out of the car and closed the door. "And what about the dwarfs? Where do they live?"

When Billy walked into his room, he closed the door behind him and put a record on the phonograph: "Dream" by the Pied Pipers. He shed his clothes as if they were heavy weights. He hung his coat on the lowered bar in his closet. He undid his tie and pulled it from his shirt, tossing it on his desk. He unfastened the buttons of his shirt and draped it over a chair. He took off his shoes and stared at the Buster Brown label inside. He took off his pants and looked down at his bowed legs.

He turned off the light and crawled into bed as the record played. He lay there, staring through the shadows on the wall. As they swayed in the moonlight, the shadows seemed to be dancing, their long gowns sweeping sheerly over the pictures on the wall. Pictures of his scout troop. Of the football team. Of him and Fibber. Of Kathy.

And seeing that picture, he turned his head into his pillow and wept.

16

After dropping Billy off, Pete and Beth drove home. It was a quarter till one by the time they coasted into the driveway. Careful not to wake the landlady, they tiptoed up the walk, gingerly turned the knob to the front door, and slipped in. While Pete was undressing, Beth put the needle of the phonograph onto the grooves of a record.

The music of "Moonlight Cocktail" filtered through the lace curtains of the open windows, which were busy unraveling moonbeams on the floor. Beth walked up behind Pete, hugging him as she softly sang along with the record.

"Congratulations, Coach," she said. He turned and their arms intertwined. "I'm so happy for you."

"They were great, weren't they? I wasn't sure they had it in 'em. But somewhere inside, it was there."

Beth kissed him as the enchantment of the music wove its seductive spell. "I've missed you," she whispered as her lips brushed against his.

"Missed you too," he whispered back.

They kissed passionately, and as the warm breeze waltzed with the curtains, they melted into each other's arms.

The next morning a slightly warmer breeze lifted the curtains of their bedroom window and softly fanned their faces. Slowly their eyes opened. Pete took a deep breath and exhaled it luxuriantly.

"Nothing ever felt as good as last night." Beth took it as a compliment. "Beatin' those guys for a shot at the championship. What a feeling."

She patted him on the hand and got up. "I'll put the coffee on."

McKinney had an off week in their schedule between the Denton game and the game with Highland Park, giving them an extra week to prepare. By Saturday afternoon, posters and banners advertising the big game were plastered all around town.

Late that afternoon Hoot and Billy borrowed the Gray Goose to do a little advertising of their own. They took a spin around the town square, checking out the scene at Gambrel's and picking up a couple of nickel Coca Colas and an order of french fries to go. They drove down a side street and barked at a stray cat over the loudspeaker. When they were through horsing around, they turned down a residential street and Billy announced: "A week from this Friday the McKinney Lions will face the Highland Park Scotties for the conference title, so mark your calendar, and let's all turn out at Newsome Stadium to help our Lions claim that championship trophy."

As they drove north on Kentucky Avenue, they spotted some good-looking junior-high girls and whistled at them over the speaker. By the time they had crisscrossed the residential areas off the town square, it was dark. While driving toward Pete's house to return the car, their headlights whipped across the back of a teenager walking down the street. As they passed him, Billy looked back.

"It's Cheetah." Hoot hit the brakes, and Billy called out over the speaker, "Need a ride?"

Cheetah caught up with them and opened the back door. "Hey, thanks."

Billy sneezed and took a handkerchief from his pocket to wipe his nose.

"You boys out for a little joyride?"

"Nah," said Hoot, "we been workin'."

"Wanna go on one?"

Billy wasn't so sure they did. "It's gettin' late and we told Coach we would—"

"Where to?" asked Hoot.

"The Rockpit."

The Rockpit was the gravel quarry outside of town. It was where innocence went in McKinney when it wanted to get lost. But, more often than admitted, although each weekend it wandered a little farther away from home, it seldom got lost.

"Cut off the lights," said Cheetah as they drove up the road leading to the quarry. Hoot turned them off and strained over the steering wheel to see ahead. As the car crept over the road, its tires crunched the gravel beneath it.

"Got the speaker stoked up?" asked Cheetah.

"All set," Billy said.

The car turned the corner, and they saw a half dozen cars parked a discreet distance apart.

"Now?" whispered Hoot.

"Not yet; hand me the speaker." The car coasted by quietly, and they could see several of the couples lost in each other's arms.

"Now," whispered Cheetah. Hoot hit the lights. "Police!" Cheetah called out over the loudspeaker. "You're all under arrest! Come out with your hands up!"

The three howled with laughter as the rending sound of speakers split the seamless night, tearing each couple from their embrace. Hoot jammed the stick in gear and peeled out, spinning doughnuts as a centripetal spray of gravel drizzled onto the parked cars. Horns blared. The Chevy spun out of control and lurched to a stop, throwing a beam over the hood of a new Studebaker. The headlight revealed Kathy, huddling in the arms of her date in a hurried attempt to hide her bare shoulders.

"Let's get outta here," Billy said. He lunged at the stick shift. "Come on, let's go!"

"Okay, okay."

Hoot stomped the pedal, and they fishtailed out of the parking area, skidding around the corner. Hoot and Cheetah rolled with laughter, but Billy just sat in the front seat, staring out his window.

The laughter abated when Billy reached over and turned on the radio. "Better be gettin' the Goose back home," he said as he blew his nose into his handkerchief.

"Just quarter till," said Hoot.

"We said we'd have it back early."

"How 'bout we take one spin around the school 'fore we call it a night, whaddya say?" said Cheetah.

"I dunno."

The car approached the darkened campus of the high school. As it skirted the parking lot, its headlights shone on an empty car with a Highland Park decal on the back window. When they pulled up beside it, the headlights froze five boys who were hoisting a sheet up the flagpole. It was already halfway up and unfurled lazily in the evening breeze:

Highland Park
District Champions
1946

"Let's get 'em," said Cheetah.

"You lost your marbles? There's five of 'em," said Hoot.

But Cheetah had already thrown open his door and was on the way out.

"You boys needin' directions back to Dallas?" said Cheetah.

Billy and Hoot jumped out of the car. When the five saw Billy, they snickered among themselves.

"Come on, Cheetah," said Billy. "Get back in the car."
Cheetah? the one smart aleck said. "They call ya that
'cause you're fast, or'd they name ya after that chim–pan–zee
in Tarzan?" The comment sparked a laugh from the Highland
Park boys.

Hoot whispered to Cheetah. "Ya know what Coach said
if he finds out you been fightin' again."

"He's startin' you, and you're gonna risk that for some
street fight? He'll bench you the whole game, and you know
he'll do it," scolded Billy.

Reluctantly, Cheetah turned and started toward the car.

"Must be 'cause you're fast," the one boy taunted.
"Looks like you're walkin' your chimp."

Cheetah stopped in his tracks.

"Forget it; let's just go," said Billy.

Cheetah turned, his teeth gritted, and walked up to
them.

"Apologize."

"Sorry, shorty." As they laughed among themselves,
Cheetah hit the boy with a devastating uppercut that sent him
reeling. The four others jumped him. Hoot and Billy rushed
to his aid. Hoot peeled one of the boys off of him and took a
swing. As it happened, he peeled off the wrong boy, who,
after ducking the swing, leveled him with a hard right. Billy
stomped on one of the boy's shoes, kicked the other in the
shin and punched the kneecap of the third. The painful
distractions gave Cheetah just enough time to slug each one
and send them falling to the ground. The remaining boy, the
one who had hit Hoot, squared off against Cheetah, lifting
his guard. But before he could throw his punch, Hoot
blindsided him and planted a cauliflower on the boy's ear that
sent him stumbling sideways.

The unspoken consensus among the Dallas boys was
that they had seen enough of McKinney for one night. They
backed away, staggering. One held a swelling ear; one, a

bruised cheek; another, a bloodied nose; another, an aching jaw; still another, a throbbing foot.

"Highway 75, south," said Cheetah, pointing directions. They started their retreat when Cheetah stepped in front of the one boy. "You're forgettin' somethin'."

"Let'm go," said Billy. But Cheetah ignored him.

"You're gonna feel better gittin' it off your chest." The boy made brief eye contact with Billy. "From the heart," said Cheetah. "Don't mean nuthin' unless it's from the heart."

"Sorry."

"His name's Billy."

"Sorry, Billy."

Cheetah came closer and looked into the boy's face. "I can tell you're feelin' better already."

The boys tumbled into their car and sped off, laying a streak of rubber behind them.

"See you boys in a couple of weeks!" hollered Hoot, then felt his hand to see if it was broken. "Bunch o' hardheads."

By the time they drove the car back to Pete's, it was later than they thought. They had a little explaining to do, especially about Hoot's swollen jaw, but Cheetah found an agile explanation that stretched the truth just far enough to be believable but short of an out-and-out lie. Pete offered to take them home, but they were afraid the truth might slip out and rear its ugly head if they weren't careful, so they opted to walk instead, offering lame excuses like "Enjoyin' the night air" or "Needin' the exercise."

They walked together until they came to the corner of Morris and Louisiana. Hoot turned left at the intersection and waved good-bye.

Billy and Cheetah continued down the lamp-lit street, their conversation punctuated by the tossing of a rock or the kicking of an occasional Coke bottle. Cheetah's intersection finally came up, and they stopped under the streetlight, laughing.

"They looked like they were knee-walkin' drunk, didn't they?" said Cheetah.

Billy nodded. "Say, thanks for takin' up for me."

"Forget it." Billy coughed as they went their separate ways. "Take care of that cold."

"I will. Say—"

"Yeah."

"We made a pretty good team back there, didn't we?"

"A *great* team."

Billy waved. "See ya Monday in English."

"So long."

Billy walked down the sidewalk to his house. Fibber was lying on the front porch, waiting up for him. As soon as he saw Billy, his ears spiked the air. He sprang to his feet and stood there, his tail eager and hopeful, but waiting for Billy to make the first move.

"Here, boy." And Fibber came running. He jumped on him and knocked him to the ground. "Whoa, boy. Easy, easy."

17

Monday morning Beth had just put a load in the wash when the machine started to clank against its casing. She ran to the kitchen, panicked to see it sloshing suds everywhere. She reached for a mop, but the faster she mopped, the more the suds frothed onto the floor. She dropped the mop and tried to steady the machine, but the washer kept chugging away. She wrapped her arms around it to muffle the noise so it wouldn't rouse the landlady. But it was too late. In walked a roused landlady, storming through the kitchen, without so much as a knock on the door. "Whaddya washin', your husband's toolbox?" she hollered.

"It just started doing that. I don't know what's wrong."

Sue reached a broom handle down the wall and jerked the plug from the electrical outlet. The machine went still, and the room was suddenly quiet. "What's wrong is, ya need to get out o' the antique business and git that husband o' yers to buy ya a decent washer."

That night, before Beth cleared the dinner dishes, Pete sat at the table, reading the newspaper. He was looking in the sports section at an ad for new tires. The four on the Chevy were bald, and it was about time to change them out.

"Sue stopped by today," Beth said, trying to make conversation through the curtain of newsprint.

"Ya don't say," he muttered. The advertisement boasted

of whitewalls for twelve dollars each. Of course, blackwalls were all he needed. Dollar cheaper. *Times four, it adds up,* he thought to himself.

"Wanna know why she came over?" she asked.

"Uh huh." *Let's see,* he figured, *that's forty-four dollars, not counting stems and mounting.* Of course, he could get by without stems. He did last time, and they're no worse for the wear. Still, with mounting, that'd be pretty near fifty dollars.

"The washing machine broke down, that's why."

"Mm—hm." *Fifty dollars for new tires,* he thought. He'd have to go to retreads. But still, retreads would come to about twenty dollars for a set. Twenty *unbudgeted* dollars.

"She said I need to get that husband of mine to buy me a new washer and get out of the antique business."

He lowered his paper and looked at her seriously. "Why in the world do you want to get into the antique business?"

"The washing machine broke."

He became suddenly attentive. "Broke what?"

"Sounded like everything."

"I'll have Billy take a look at it."

Without warning, the door flew open, and in walked Sue. "Well, what's he gonna do?"

"He's gonna try to get it fixed."

"It ain't worth fixin', any fool could see that. M'papa used to always say, 'You buy secondhand, you're buyin' somebody else's troubles.'"

Pete got up and ushered Sue out the door. "Thanks for stoppin' by, Sue; we appreciate your concern. And we'll let you know how the repairs turn out." Once she was gone, Pete turned to Beth. "We gotta get a latch on that door."

As Sue walked down the walkway, she passed Ted Murphy, who was walking up it.

"A decent husband would buy his wife a washer," she complained.

"A decent apartment would come with one," he replied.

"Men, humph. You're all cut out of the same bolt of cloth."

As she walked away in a huff, Pete welcome Ted inside.

"Evenin', Pete, Beth."

"Come on in," said Pete.

"Sit down, please," said Beth.

"Can't stay. Just dropped by to give ya this." He pulled an envelope out of his pocket and handed it to Pete.

"I don't understa—"

"Open it."

Pete opened the envelope. "There's, there's a hundred dollars here."

"Just a little somethin' to tide ya over; we know things are tight."

"Ted, you don't have that kind of money," said Pete.

"No," he said, smiling, "but the men at the barber shop do. I passed the hat around and that's what fell into it."

After Ted left, Pete counted the money again. "Why, with a hundred dollars we could buy a new set of tires and have enough left over to get that washer of yours fixed."

Beth took the envelope from his hand. "With a hundred dollars we could get a new washer and have enough left over to get that car of yours a set of retreads."

Monday after practice they went to an appliance store in Dallas in response to an ad they saw in the paper.

"We were wantin' to look at some washing machines," Pete told the salesman.

"Well, you came to the right place," the man replied.

"Ours broke down," explained Beth.

"Nuthin' gets a woman down in the dumps faster than a broke-down washer—am I right or am I right?"

Beth nodded.

"Less'n it's a backed-up septic tank—am I right or am I right?"

"You're right."

"We were wantin' to see what you had on special," said Pete.

"Just so has it, I got a mismatched pair of Hamiltons. The washer is top of the line. Advertised right here in *House Beautiful*."

When he picked up the magazine to show them, a copy of the *Dallas Times Herald* was revealed underneath it. Pete studied the ad as Beth looked down at the headlines of the sports page: HIGHLAND PARK EXPECTED TO WALK AWAY WITH ITS THIRD CONSECUTIVE TITLE. As she stewed over the arrogance of those words, the salesman was putting a sharp pencil to his mental arithmetic.

"Let it go for, say, well, now, I'm givin' it away so don't go breathin' this around town—" He whispered, "Seventy-nine, ninety-nine." The salesman checked her reaction, which wasn't good. "Of course, that includes tax." He tried again to read her reaction, which was getting worse by the second. "And delivery." She turned to Pete, starting to seethe over the headlines. "And a service policy." He could sense the sale slipping away from him. "What do I have to do, come over and fold your clothes?"

"We were really hopin' for something a little cheaper," said Pete. "We've got to buy some tires too."

"I could sell ya somethin' cheaper; I could do that. But ya know what they say, 'you get what you pay for'—am I right or am I right?"

"You're right," said Beth, "you're just too expensive." She was getting a little testy now. "Can my husband and I have a minute, alone?"

"Sure, sure, you two put your heads together, come up with a price you can live with, make me an offer, and I'll see what I can do to help you good folks. That's what I'm here for." He smiled broadly and backed away a few steps.

175

"I don't think we ought to get the washer," Beth whispered.

"He's just a big-city salesman; don't let him bother you."

"I heard you talking on the phone the other night about the team's needing helmets." Pete nodded. "How many helmets would a hundred dollars buy?"

The next day Ted Murphy was mustering up the courage to ask Miss Caulfield to the Highland Park game. He waited until she had a break in her schedule, then went to the boys' bathroom to comb his hair and neaten himself up first.

He stood in front of the mirror, pressing his face close to see if there was anything that was fixable. He touched the tip of his finger to his mouth and with a dab of saliva rubbed the last remnant of lunch from the corner of his mouth. He twirled back an curlicue of hair that lay coiled over his ear, then yanked an unsightly one sprouting from the top of that ear.

He cleared his throat and practiced his delivery. "We play Highland Park Friday week, and I was wonderin' if you were plannin' on goin'—" He stopped himself, shaking his head in disgust. He cleared his throat again and took another pass at it. "As you know, we play Highland Park—"

From behind him in a closed stall the toilet flushed. Murphy jerked down a paper towel and pretended to be cleaning out the sink when a sophomore boy emerged from the stall.

"I was tryin' to get yer attention in there," scolded Murphy. "Ya know we play Highland Park next week for the district championship, don't ya?"

"Yes, sir, I do." The boy, somewhat awkwardly, reached for the faucet handle and washed his hands.

"Well, yer gonna be there, aren't ya?"

"I was plannin' on it." The boy hurriedly dried his hands with a paper towel.

"It's important we have a good turnout," said Murphy as he wiped down the sink.

"I'll be there," said the boy.

"We can count on ya then?"

"Yessir."

"Good."

Murphy walked down the hall, still rehearsing his lines and still bungling them. Finally, he told himself that when he got to her room, he would just knock, and when she invited him in, that would be his cue and that's when he would ask her and whatever came out of his mouth would just have to do. The plan emboldened him, and his stride grew brisk and confident. When he came to her room, he took a deep breath and rapped on the door frame.

"Oh, Ted—hi. Come in."

"You wouldn't want to come to the Highland Park game with me by any chance, would you?"

"I'd love to."

"Well, maybe we could make it some other time then." He turned to go when she called out to him.

"I'd love to go with you to the game."

"You would?" He turned. "I mean, we can count on you then?"

Miss Caulfield fought back a smile. "Yes."

"Good."

The bell rang, and in Pete's American history class all the students had taken their seats. He opened his grade book and called roll.

"Abbot?"

"Here."

"Billingsworth?"

"Here."

"Button?" There was no answer, and Pete looked up to see Billy's vacant desk. "Billy absent again?"

"He wasn't in first period," said Hoot.

"Prob'ly just doggin' it," said Cheetah.

"Go down to the office, Hoot, and call his home, will ya?"

Hoot returned to class and talked to Pete in hushed tones. "He's in the hospital."

"Hospital? How come?"

"I dunno. Neighbor lady who was house sittin' said his grandparents took him this mornin'; didn't know what for, just that it was an emergency."

Pete took his keys from his pocket and gave them to Hoot. "Go see how he's doin'." Hoot started for the door, and Cheetah got up from his desk. "Can I go with him, Coach?"

Pete nodded. "Call me when you find out something."

Once at the hospital, Cheetah and Hoot looked timidly around the lobby and down the endless hallways of white. They saw an old woman on a gurney being fed by a bulbous I.V. that looked to them like a giant mosquito hovering above her, and they recoiled at the sight. The smell of medicines mingling antiseptically in the air made their stomachs feel a little queasy, and the sound of someone moaning down the hall made them feel even worse.

"May I help you?" asked a woman in a crisp white uniform at the information desk.

"Uh, we were lookin' for a friend o' ours," said Cheetah.

"His name?"

"Button, Billy Button. Might be listed as William," Hoot said nervously.

She looked at her roster. "Room 315, but he can't have visitors."

"How come?" asked Cheetah.

"I don't know. You'll have to talk to the head nurse on the third floor."

They started getting really nervous now. They went to

the elevator and Cheetah punched the button, but the elevator didn't respond. He punched the button again and again. He looked around and spotted the sign for the stairs. They hurdled up the steps and, with their hearts pounding in their throats, arrived on the third floor. The nurses' station was like Grand Central, women in white shuttling back and forth, reading charts, measuring out pills, filling syringes.

"Excuse me," said Cheetah to the nurse who was studying a chart. "Excuse me, ma'am."

The woman looked up. "Yes."

She directed them to the waiting room where Mr. and Mrs. Button were keeping vigil. It was there they learned of Billy's condition.

They hurried to the pay phone. Cheetah dug into his jeans for a nickel and slipped it into the slot. "Two- six- two," he said and waited for the operator to make the connection. "Hello. I need ya to get Coach Williams. It's an emergency."

The office worker hurried to Pete's history class where he was mapping out the battle of Little Big Horn. When the girl interrupted his class, he chalked on the board, *Read pages 72– 80.*

Once in the office he picked up the phone. "This is Coach Williams."

"Coach." Cheetah's voice faltered. "You gotta get down here; you gotta get down here right away."

Pete picked up the broken fragments of the boy's sentences and pieced together Billy's condition. When Cheetah finally finished, Pete hung up and relayed the news to the superintendent.

The superintendent interrupted classes with three dongs over the loudspeaker. "I've just received some tragic news about one of our students. This morning Billy Button suffered a cerebral hemorrhage and was taken to the county hospital, where he is in critical condition. Classes will be dismissed for the rest of the day for any wanting to go to the hospital. Please remember him and his family in your prayers."

The P.A. went mute. The news was met with stunned silence. Some sat in their desks, paralyzed by the sudden impact of the news. Some turned to each other in a chatty state of disbelief: *Billy? Our Billy? The manager? What's a cerebral hemorrhage? He seemed fine last week. He was at the dance the other night, wasn't he? I can't believe it; I just can't believe it.*

Pete floored the superintendent's car down the road to the hospital, eddies of brittle leaves curling skyward in its wake. When he arrived there, he swerved into the parking lot and screeched to a stop.

The elevator opened at the nurses' station. He looked down the hall and saw Cheetah and Hoot standing outside Billy's room.

"How is he?"

"Don't know; doctor's in there with him now," said Cheetah.

"How did it happen?"

"He was at home and just passed out," said Hoot.

A doctor came out, along with a nurse who held a tray cluttered with medical paraphernalia.

"How is he?" asked Pete.

"We've given him a spinal tap to relieve the pressure. It's a common problem with hemorrhages—fluid build-up. Causes pressure on the brain. If you don't shunt off some of the fluid, it can trigger convulsions. We've taken out as much as we possibly can—"

"How does it look?"

"Not good."

"Can I see him? I'm his coach."

"Go ahead, but he won't be able to recognize you; he's in a coma."

Pete entered the room where the venetian blinds had cut

the sun into strips of light. He looked at Billy, lying quietly in the bed, secured tightly by a blanket that was anchored by taut hospital corners. He walked over to him and gripped the raised rails. He studied his face for signs of consciousness. There were none.

"Billy. Can you hear me?" Pete ran his hand in front of the boy's eyes. Not so much as a blink. He took his hand and stroked his arm.

After a few moments, Pete walked around the room, running his hand over his face, as if searching their contours for some explanation. He bent a blind and looked down at the lawn below. Cars started pulling up to the curb, and doors opened to unload piles of high-school kids onto the sidewalk. Byron. Gill. Kathy. Connie Sue. Freight Train. Before long the entire student body had assembled on the lawn, fanning out from the front doors. They clustered together in threes and fours, friends finding friends, clinging to each other, hoping, praying.

Short bursts of optimism broke through the gloom: stories of elderly relatives who had survived similar ordeals; rays of hope about the competency of the hospital staff; somebody beaming on about the miracles of modern medicine.

Few of those gathered on that lawn had ever had a close brush with death. Several had experienced the demise of an ailing grandparent or a casual acquaintance of the family that had not returned from the war or news in a letter of a distant relative who had passed on. That was about as close as any of them had come. But now death was at their door, knocking for one of them. And that knock shook the latch that gave security to their lives.

News of Billy's condition swept through the crowd, rustling emotions. A light drizzle of tears followed; a drop here, furtively wiped away; another there, sniffed back.

Pete took Billy's hand and prayed, prayed with all the

strength he had in him. As he held his hand, he felt a flicker of life pass through it. Then another. He looked up to see a flutter from Billy's eyelashes. He gripped harder and prayed harder, feeling the life flow from his body to Billy's. He looked up at him hopefully.

Billy's face began to twitch. The twitching grew more violent until the rails clattered against the bed frame.

"Nurse! Doctor! Somebody help!"

Hoot threw open the door. Cheetah rushed in to help while Hoot yelled down the hall, "We need some help down here, quick!"

Pete pressed himself against Billy's body, trying to constrain it. He grappled to hold down his arms, crying out as he pushed his head against the boy's chest: "Oh God, please help him, God, please, God."

Hoot yelled at the nurses, "HURRY!"

A nurse ran through the door, followed by a blur of white, a doctor and several nurses rushing to the bedside, each grabbing a flailing appendage and wrestling it to the bed.

"He's biting his tongue!" the doctor shouted. "Get something between his teeth!" A nurse grabbed a handful of tongue depressors from her pocket. The two doctors tried to pry his mouth open and slide a couple of the depressors in, but Billy's jaws snapped them in two.

"He's choking; turn him," ordered the doctor. They turned him on his side. He retched and coughed. Then his body grew limp.

"Clear the airway!"

The other doctor dug his hand down Billy's mouth to clear it of any foreign matter.

"It's clear," he said, and they slowly turned him, letting him rest on his back. The nurses relaxed their hold. The doctor thrust his hand onto the carotid artery on Billy's neck. No pulse. He checked Billy's pupils. They were fixed. And he gently closed the boy's eyelids.

Pete released his grip on Billy's arm, where deep, red gouges marked the struggle to hold on to his life. Cheetah was still clutching Billy's leg. Pete backed away and bumped against the wall. The doctors and nurses talked among themselves, but it was all just a slur of sounds to him.

He walked out of the room. A pair of footsteps echoed toward him. He lifted his head. Billy's grandparents, running from the waiting room. They stopped and saw the red rims of his pooling eyes. He reached out and gathered them to himself, and the three of them clung to each other desperately and wept.

Ten minutes later the elevator doors on the ground floor opened to reveal Pete, a lobby full of faces staring back at him.

"How's he doin'?" asked Byron.

Pete looked at him. His red and puffy eyes told everyone in the lobby what his trembling mouth couldn't. He shook his head.

"Oh, no," he sobbed, his chest heaving convulsively as he buried his face into Gill's shoulder.

18

The funeral was held Saturday morning. The white clapboard church was packed, and three hundred people crowded the grounds outside. Inside, the wooden pews kept everyone's eyes focused on the front of the sanctuary. There Billy lay at rest in a child's casket. The bottom half of the casket was festooned with roses and a delicate filigree of ferns. The cover on the top half was raised. A few of the older people, those more accustomed to the protocols of grief, walked down the aisle and paused in front of the casket. Most of the high school students didn't. The few who did, wept—their muffled tears ascending plaintively to join with the somber chords of the organ prelude.

When the prelude ended, the organist played the introduction to "Rock of Ages." This cued Byron and two other football players who got up from the front pew and took their place on the chancel. The trio took a deep breath and sang:

> *Rock of Ages, cleft for me,*
> *Let me hide myself in Thee!*

The one boy's lip quivered from the very first word, and after a few notes he couldn't go on.

> *Let the water and the blood*
> *From Thy riven side which flowed, . . .*

The other boy's voice began to falter a few notes later, tears streaming down his face. Before long his voice trailed off into silence, leaving Byron to finish the stanza alone.

> *Be of sin the double cure,*
> *Cleanse me from its guilt and power.*

His voice struggled to keep up with the organ, missing a word or two.

> *Not the labors of my hands*
> *Can fulfill Thy Law's demands;*
> *Could my zeal no respite know,*
> *Could my tears—*

Byron couldn't go on. The organ held a note for him to catch up. When it was obvious Byron wasn't going to recover, Cheetah, sitting a couple of pews from the front, picked up the line and started to sing.

> *—forever flow,*
> *Thou must save, and Thou alone.*
> *All for sin could not atone;*

Byron took a deep breath and somehow found the strength to continue. On the next stanza the organ played louder.

> *Nothing in my hand I bring;*
> *Simply to Thy cross I cling;*

First it was only Cheetah and Byron singing, then one by one the others joined in. Hoot. Then Gill. Then Freight Train. Then all the other football players.

> *Naked, come to Thee for dress;*
> *Helpless, look to Thee for grace;*
> *Foul, I to the fountain fly;*
> *Wash me, Saviour, or I die!*

By the final stanza, everyone in the church joined in.

While I draw this fleeting breath,
While my eye-strings close in death,—
When I soar through tracts unknown;
See Thee on Thy Judgment Throne;—
Rock of Ages, cleft for me,
Let me hide myself in Thee.

After Reverend Chattsworth finished his eulogy, hundreds of mourners quietly filed out of the old church, got into their cars, and fell in line behind the hearse. The long caravan of headlights trailed the hearse on its ride to the gravesite.

Pete and Beth drove in their car with Miss Caulfield and Murphy in the backseat. "The doctor said it's a weak blood vessel that starts bleeding in the brain," said Pete. "Something like a weak spot in an inner tube. You may never have any trouble with it, and then one day it bubbles out and bursts—just like that. Sometimes something sets it off—doctor said his cold might have had something to do with it—but he didn't know for sure."

Kathy, Connie Sue, and Mary Ellen all rode together. All the way to the gravesite none of them said a word.

Behind them was Willard Kincaid's car, filled with members of the school board.

Bob and Lynell Jeffers drove with Byron and Hoot in the backseat. Byron looked out his window and, with no more tears inside him left to cry, took private inventory of his loss. Hoot rested his head against the seat and stared at the low ceiling of the car, his mouth dry and pasty, an aching lump lodged in his throat.

Uncle Clyde drove Cheetah and his mother and Gill in his old jalopy. There was a long stretch of silence before Gill spoke up. "Dudn't seem fair, does it? Like some runt pig gettin' shunned by its mama. Seems like she oughta be the one to push the others away and take up for it so the little'n could get a full teat. But she don't. Dudn't seem right, but she don't."

19

The Monday after the funeral was quiet at school as grief for Billy turned inward. Even between classes when the clatter of lockers normally echoed through the halls, there was no loud talk or laughter or hollered greetings. And despite the posterboard signs, there was no talk about Friday night's game with Highland Park.

In Miss Caulfield's class Byron stared at Billy's empty desk, deep in thought. To the other side of the empty desk sat Cheetah, mindlessly turning his pencil end over end. He looked over at Billy's desk, then up at Byron. And over that empty desk, their eyes, drained of all malice, met.

In the locker room Gill walked past a few towels on the floor. Normally he would have left them for the managers, but he stopped, picked them up, and dropped them into the hamper.

At noon Hoot ate his lunch in the equipment cage, alone, staring at the legacy of efficiency that Billy had left. His eyes perused the neatly arranged shelves and cabinets and finally came to rest on Billy's paddle, hanging dormant on a hook.

Calisthenics that afternoon were sluggish, everyone running on empty. Pete blew his whistle, and the boys slowly circled around him. Fibber came too, as if he were one of them. Cheetah sat next to him and petted him. Fibber looked up. Cheetah smiled and rubbed him behind his ears, something Fibber had always liked.

"What happened last week makes Friday's game seem pretty unimportant," said Pete. . . . "But Highland Park'll be comin' to town, and comin' ready to play. Best we can, we need to be ready too. . . . We worked hard for this, to be where we are. I don't think Billy would want us lettin' up now, do you?" There was a sprinkling of "nosirs" and an almost imperceptible shaking of heads.

After practice, everyone went home quietly. Byron was the last one out of the showers and the only one left in the locker room. As he tied his shoes, he noticed a textbook on the bench. He picked it up and opened it. "John Henry Brown" was scrawled on the inside cover. He put it down, then changed his mind and took it with him.

It was dusk by the time he drove his father's car to the Browns' house. He creaked open the gate of the rickety picket fence and walked up the porch. He rapped a couple of polite knocks on the screen door. Mrs. Brown came to the door, drying his hands on a dishtowel.

"Well hello, Byron."

"Howdy, Mrs. Brown. Is Cheetah home?"

"He went for a walk. Should be back in about a half hour, when supper's on."

He opened the screen and tried to hand her the book. "He left this in the locker room."

"Mighty sweet of ya to drop it by." She paused a second, then handed the book back. "Why don't you give it to him? He went in the direction of the mill. I imagine he'd welcome the company."

Byron drove to the industrial sprawl of white buildings that made up the Texas Textile Mill. The workers had all gone home for the day, and the mill stood silent and empty. Cheetah stood holding a handful of rocks as Byron drove up. Sweat poured from his face, and his shirt was dripping wet.

He gritted his teeth as he threw a rock through one of the high windows, shattering it.

Byron looked up and saw a row of windows broken out. "What are you doin'?"

"Just my way of dealin' with things."

"I, uh, brought your English book." The next rock was low and clanked against the sheet metal wall. "You left it in the locker room."

Cheetah reached over and took the book. "Didn't need to drive it all the way out here. Not like it'd've been the first time I didn't do my homework." He reared back and hurled another rock, breaking still another window. "But thanks."

Byron nodded, put the stick on the steering column in reverse. "So long."

"Hey, can I bum a ride?"

"Sure."

Byron pulled up in front of Cheetah's house, put the car in park, and stared out the windshield. "It happened so quick . . . no warnin', nothin'. Like that tornado that tore through here last spring. Everything peaceful and calm, just another day, and then *bam,* it hit." He paused, then looked at Cheetah. "He was my best friend . . . since seventh grade. Whenever I was down, he'd always have a way of pickin' me up; ya know how he was, those little pep talks of his." He ran his hand over the steering wheel, trying to generate strength for his words. "Just wish I could've let him know how much he meant to me. I never told him that. All I talked to him about, and I never talked about that."

The next day after workout Byron knocked on the door to Pete's office.

"Come in."

Byron walked in, a little nervous. "Got a minute, Coach?"

He nodded. "Have a seat."

"It was always a big thing to Button to beat Highland Park; I mean, it was to all of us, but 'specially to him." There was a short pause before he got the courage to make his request. "We want to dedicate the game to Billy."

Pete leaned forward. "Close the door." Byron pulled it closed. "I know you want to do something for Billy, something special, but maybe this isn't the best way to do it."

"We all talked it over, and everybody feels the same way."

"What happens if you *don't* win it for Billy? What then? How's it gonna affect the team? The school?"

"We'll be ready."

Pete thought hard before he gave his answer. "I wish you wouldn't do it . . . but I won't tell you no."

When Byron came out of his office, the whole squad was looking at him in anticipation of Pete's answer. "He said yes."

"Huddle up a minute," said Byron. The boys closed ranks around him. "There's a lot of things we all felt for Billy; lot of things if he were here we'd want to tell him. But he isn't, so we'll need to say what we want to say Friday night."

For the remainder of the week the boys divided up and met each night in each other's dens and garages and bedrooms. The linemen met at Herman Tucker's house to discuss Highland Park's line and to walk through their blocking assignments. The backs met at Freight Train's house to go over offensive strategy. Thursday night the entire team came to Byron's house for a final team meeting in his attic bedroom. The mood was serious. No joking around. No idle talk. They closed the meeting in prayer, and those that wanted to, said a few words.

"Dear Lord God Almighty, Maker of Heaven and Earth—" Cheetah stopped himself and looked up. "Can I start over?" Several of the boys nodded. "We all loved Billy, Lord. He taped our ankles, rubbed our cramps, gave us a pat on the back when we needed it . . . and busted our tails when we needed that. . . ."

"We were nuthin' a year ago," prayed Gill, "and now we're somethin'—we're a team. . . ."

"It's not the glory we're after, God," prayed Byron. "It's not for us. It's for Billy. . . ."

20

Friday while Beth was drinking a second cup of morning coffee, she heard a knock. She walked to the screen door and saw her landlady standing there.

"Good morning, Sue."

The old woman's face had softened and her voice had grown kind. "I was meanin' to come by earlier. I just wanted to say how sorry I am about the boy who died, the manager. Billy was his name?"

Beth nodded. "Thank you."

"How's your husband taking it?"

"Pretty hard. It was hard on everybody." She paused. "Listen, you wanna come in for some coffee?"

"I really don't have the—"

"Oh, come on," she coaxed as she unlatched the screen door and opened it. "I've already got it made."

"I can't stay long." She came in and had some coffee. She talked about her husband's death twenty years ago and the sadness of seeing her friends die off, one by one, and the loneliness of being the last of them to die. After an hour had slowly reminisced by, Beth took her book of poetry from the shelf and read aloud.

> *This is the Hour of Lead—*
> *Remembered, if outlived,*
> *As freezing persons, recollect the Snow—*

First—Chill—then Stupor—
Then the letting go.

"Who was it wrote that?" Sue asked.

"Emily Dickinson."

"Mind if I borrow it?"

"No. Go ahead."

"I'll have it back to you—"

"There's no hurry. Take the time and enjoy her. She's been like a friend to me, and I'm delighted to share her."

"Thank you. Well, I best be goin'. I suppose you've got a lot to do before the game tonight."

"Say," Beth said, the thought suddenly coming to her, "why don't you come with me?"

"To the game?" Beth nodded. "It's been twenty-five years since I've been to a football game, not since before Horace died—"

"It'll do you good to get out."

"It might at that. Besides," she said with a smile. "I'd like to see what that husband of yours does for a living."

That husband of hers was at his office desk, talking on the phone to a sporting-goods store in Dallas.

"Well how many do you have?"

There was a rap on the door.

"Come in," he said, holding his hand over the mouthpiece.

"No, we can't wait till you get another shipment in; we need the helmets today. That's right; this afternoon at the latest."

A deliveryman with a clipboard entered his office. "Got a delivery for Coach Pete Williams."

He stood up as he saw two other men bringing boxes into the locker room. "Delivery for what?"

"Uniforms. Ordered last week by—" He looked at the shipping order. "—a Willard Kincaid. Said it had to be delivered by noon today at the latest, or it was 'no sale.' " He looked at his watch. "Ten forty-five. Sign at the bottom." Pete spoke into the phone, "Can you hold on?" He scribbled his signature across the delivery slip and tore open one of the boxes. He lifted out a jersey. It had a muted gold background with deep blue numbers and three matching bands running horizontally around the upper arms. He looked in another box and found matching gold pants. In another box he found the helmets, thick leather, padded inside; the outside, a polished blue with a gold stripe running down the middle.

Pete went back to the phone. "I won't be needin' those helmets after all."

At lunch Pete sat in the boiler room with Murphy, bouncing a few ideas off the old mentor, talking through a few final bits of strategy. Pete scribbled a play on his lunch sack, but Murphy just sat back and shook his head.

"Ya don't win a game like this with razzle-dazzle."

Pete crumpled up the sack and tossed it into the open mouth of the incinerator. "It's just that I'm afraid how the boys are gonna take it if they lose. I've never seen 'em this keyed-up before."

"What makes ya think they're gonna lose?"

"They got us out-manned, out-coached."

"Ya don't win a game—not a game like this anyway—by how good ya are . . . or how smart. Ya win it by how much heart is in those eleven boys ya put on that field. Hide and watch, tonight they're gonna show how much heart they got. And I think them city folks from Dallas are gonna get a lesson in what the game of football is really all about."

After lunch, classes let out for the pep rally. The yell leaders had been up till midnight decorating the auditorium. The place reverberated with spirit, the band playing the fight song while students streamed through the doorway. The football team stood in the first row, dressed in their suit pants, but instead of coats and ties, they all wore their new jerseys. When the fight song ended, the student body applauded and then took their seats.

The head yell leader spoke into the microphone and addressed the team: "Come on, Lions, stand up and show us your colors."

The team stood up and turned around, and the yell leader rallied the audience: "Let's hear it for the blue and gold!" The auditorium was a sudden rush of emotion as the students jumped to their feet and cheered. The yell leaders all took their megaphones and whipped the crowd into a frothing frenzy:

"What are we going to do tonight?"

"Beat Highland Park!" yelled the audience in reply.

"WHAT?"

"BEAT HIGHLAND PARK!"

"LOUDER!"

"BEAT HIGHLAND PARK!"

At Newsome Stadium that night the cheerleaders continued to work the crowd.

"WE CAN'T HEAR YOU!"

"BEAT HIGHLAND PARK!"

Overhead a jumble of clouds floated low in the sky, filling the air with the promise of rain. The crowd was wrapped in their sweaters and blankets, their thermoses full of hot coffee and their umbrellas sheathed closely at hand.

The bleachers were thick with smells from the concession stand that the Quarterback Club operated: hot dogs warming up buns that smelled boldly of mustard and onions and relish; peanuts incubating aromatically in their shells; hot popcorn seething with butter; vapor trails of black coffee floating warmly down rows of bundled fans.

The row that held the Brown household was especially thick with concession-stand smells, several of the old men having dipped into their savings to savor the full experience of this night. Nadine passed a thermos of coffee down the row, and Uncle Clyde helped Sydney open a sack of roasted peanuts, lightening it by two or three for his efforts.

Huddled up higher in the stands was the Thompson family, all fourteen of them. Most of the kids had never seen Gill play before. They were google-eyed by the spectacle of it all, sitting on the edges of their seats, craning their necks to see the yell leaders perform on the grassy margin in front of the bleachers. The yell leaders, dressed crisply in their white pleated uniforms, finished a cheer and stood in formation, waving their pom-poms in the air.

The noise in the stands ebbed a little after the last cheer, and the McKinney fans could hear Highland Park warming up in the far end zone. The sight and sounds of the well-disciplined Dallas team were impressive. Their side-straddle hops were brisk and precisely executed: *One, Two, Three, Four, One, Two, Three, Four.* Each time the *one* came around, their voices joined together like a battering ram against the wall of night air. The defending state champs had come to town, all right. And from the looks of it, from the sound of it, they had come to play, determined to bring the title back with them on the bus back to Big D. McKinney had their work cut out for them. They were outmanned all the way down the roster. Highland Park was bigger, faster, had more depth on the bench, and any of their three assistant coaches had more experience than Pete—not to mention their head coach who already had six conference crowns and a state title under his belt.

While the Scotties ran through their drills, the Lions huddled under the bleachers around Pete. There was no slapping each other on the helmets or popping one another with their shoulder pads. A predatory intensity crouched inside them, wild and instinctive. They strained to hear Pete's words, the deafening noise of the crowd almost drowning him out.

"You got your work cut out for you. They're good. Better'n Greenville. Better'n us. They're bigger, faster, tougher. But that's not what wins football games." For a few seconds the roar of the crowd subsided. "It's what's in here," he said, pointing to his heart. "And if ya go by what's in here, there isn't any better team in the state than the one I'm lookin' at right now." As he said those words, he surveyed the circle of eyes that surrounded him. He extended his hand to the middle of the huddle. One by one the boys extended theirs. The McKinney crowd was chanting to a cheer led by the yell leaders, and Pete had to shout to get himself heard: "It doesn't matter how big they are, or how fast, or how tough. If you play your hearts out, you're gonna have the edge; just remember that, you're gonna have the edge."

With a shout they threw down their hands and broke huddle. As they ran onto the field, the McKinney fans rose to their feet, their cheers coming like wind against the players' backs, lifting them.

Elaine Caulfield turned to Ted. "How do you think the boys look in their new uniforms?"

"Like champions," Ted said loudly enough for Beth to hear. Beth smiled and held up her two fingers, crossed for good luck. To the one side of her stood Lynell Jeffers, and her husband; to the other, Sue Harrelson; behind her, Willard Kincaid and his wife, the remark about the uniforms clearly pleasing him.

As the teams gathered on either sideline, the band played the prelude to the national anthem. Highland Park stood mute on the sidelines with their hands over their hearts as the national anthem was sung over the P.A. system. McKinney stood on their sidelines, proud to be Lions, proud to be wearing the blue-and-gold. As they held their helmets in their hands, their voices ascended into the night air, full of passion, full of heart, full of a dream on the threshold of fulfillment. When the anthem ended, Reverend Chattsworth gave the prayer over the P.A. system, publicly invoking the blessing of God on both teams, but privately adding a silent postscript to tilt providence a few degrees in their favor.

When the prayer concluded, Gill turned and started to put on his helmet, but his eye caught a familiar face in the crowd—Miss Caulfield's. For the brief moment their eyes met.

"Captains on the field!" called Pete through his cupped hands, and two of the senior co-captains put on their helmets, waiting for the third. "Let's go, Gill."

Then the farm boy who had almost missed his senior season put on his helmet for the most important game of his life. And by the grace of that teacher in the stands, he took his place with the other two captains and walked to the center of the field. The referees introduced them to the opposing captains. They all shook hands, and Highland Park won the coin toss, electing to receive.

McKinney lined up on their forty-yard line, spaced evenly across the width of the field, awaiting the referee's signal to put the ball in play. He blew his whistle, and the kicker put the full force of his leg into the ball.

The clock started. Forty-eight minutes, and the conference champions would be decided.

The ball sailed end over end until it finally tumbled from the mottled sky inside the ten. The deep man for the Scotties called for it, setting in motion a wall of blockers who fell back to defend him. But he had trouble finding the handle on the ball, and when he finally scooped it up, the blockers had left without him. Cheetah and the other McKinney end, who had been running down the sidelines, curled in on the runner and hammered him, nailing his numbers to the eight-yard line.

The defensive effort read like a banner spread across the

field for all the Dallas fans to read: McKinney had come to play too.

The first play from scrimmage the offense lined up in a T-formation. The Scotties ran the halfback off tackle, but he was stacked up for no gain. Second and ten, the quarterback faked the previous play and gave the ball to the fullback up the middle. A gain of two, but he had to fall forward to get that. Third and eight. The defensive secondary played up for the short pass, but Highland Park wanted to establish its running game early and handed off instead to the left half running around the right end.

Byron, playing defensive back, spotted the play unfolding and ran up to break through the interference and make the tackle. The McKinney fans cheered the defensive effort, but no fans cheered as loud or as long as Byron's parents.

The referee spotted the ball, and the announcer interpreted his signals to the waiting crowd: "A pick-up of four on the play. Fourth down and four yards to go for a first." The McKinney fans rose to their feet and cheered. Their boys had held Highland Park, held the defending state champs, forcing them to kick.

The Scotties broke huddle and lined up in punt formation. They kicked the ball from the end zone, a booming one that arched high in the air, high enough for the prevailing wind to help it along to their forty-yard line. Still, it was good field position for the Lions. The run-back netted them six yards, putting the ball on the Highland Park thirty-four.

The Lions gathered in a knot of determination, the boys all looking to Byron for their first offensive play of the game. "Freight Train over right tackle, short count, so get set—on one."

The two lines squared off. Highland Park's outweighed McKinney's by twenty-five to thirty pounds per player, but the thought of the inequity never entered the Lions' minds.

Cheetah and Gill dug in on the right side of the line, their eyes lit by some wild fire that raged deep within them.

"Hut one!" The McKinney line crashed against Highland Park like a wave against a jutting coastline. But like a hardened coastline, the defense held its position. Freight Train collided into the sheer cliffs of flesh and, unable to find so much as a fissure of an opening, changed directions. The defensive end was there, braced to make the tackle, so the determined McKinney back planted his foot and reversed his course, curling back to try the other end. By that time, though, a wall of Scotties collapsed on him. A loss of five on the play.

Second and fifteen, McKinney lined up in a spread formation. Freight Train flanked wide to the left. The ends were split. Freight Train went five yards deep and cut over the middle, but the linebacker was all over him. Cheetah ran the same pattern but faked inside and cut back to the sidelines. He got a step on his defensive man, and the ball was right there when he made his cut. He snagged it out of the air and pulled it to his chest before the defender caught up with him and pushed him out of bounds.

Nadine Brown, Uncle Clyde, Sidney, and the whole Brown household of old-age pensioners were all there in the stands, cheering like a bunch of teenagers.

The referee spotted the ball. A gain of eight on the play. Third and seven.

The next down Byron ran the same play. Dropping back to pass, he looked right, then left. All his receivers were covered. His eye caught a glimmer of daylight that Gill had opened on the right side of the line, and he sprinted through it upfield. He cut against the grain and picked up a blocker before he was finally chased out of bounds at the sixteen-yard line. The Lions had penetrated the sacred twenty-yard line that the Scotties tried so hard to defend. First and ten. The crowd went berserk.

Highland Park pulled together on the next play when a pack of Scotties sunk their teeth into McKinney's running back and buried him like a backyard bone, forcing him to fumble. They took possession of the ball on their own eighteen-yard line. After a standoff of three downs, Highland Park punted, booming the pigskin high above the lights. It took a Highland Park bounce and rolled dead, deep into McKinney territory. The battle for yardage was tough; two yards a carry, sometimes three; seldom more than that. In a persistent ground attack McKinney churned out the yards and dominated the first half of play.

By the time the half ended, the scoreboard read: McKINNEY LIONS 0—VISITORS 0.

The Lions ran off the field to the elation of the home crowd. They grouped together under the bleachers, sweaty, panting, their jerseys disheveled and grass-stained, their skin smeared with a mixture of blood, dirt, and powdered lime. The noise of the band pounded their eardrums so hard that they felt they were on the verge of exploding.

"Hand me the stat sheet," Pete said to Hoot. The boy handed him a clipboard. "We've gained sixty-eight yards to their twenty-six . . . six first downs to their one . . . and one penetration to their none. You're kickin' 'em all over the field. But we need to get on the scoreboard the second half. If we don't and it goes down to the wire in a tie, remember, we can win it on penetrations. We've got 'em beat there so far with our one penetration, so defense, dig in; don't let 'em score." A clap of thunder punctuated Pete's remarks. He looked at the boys huddled around him. "You're playing like champions, like champions. . . . Billy would've been proud. . . . You're just twenty-four minutes away from winnin'. Take it a minute at a time."

With a clap of Pete's hands, the boys shot to their feet and ran onto the field. For a moment, time seemed to stretch before them like an endless page, and the ovation they received was so forceful, so overwhelming, it seemed as if the fans were pressing them onto that page to preserve the memory of this moment forever in their minds.

The third quarter was down-and-dirty, linemen plowing up the field with their cleats, as intermittent drops of rain fell from the sky.

From the first play of the second half, the Highland Park end started to taunt Cheetah. He did it throughout the quarter, a little jab here, a jab there, just enough to break his concentration. He said things like, "You pick a lot of cotton, huh, farm boy?" or "They got indoor toilets where you go to school?" Cheetah just stonewalled him, but the boy kept digging. "Hey, I'm talkin' to you. They teach you how to talk at that hick school o' yours?" By the end of the third quarter a smattering of rain began to affect the field, the uniforms being the first to show it as they soaked in the mud. Just before the quarter ended, the Highland Park end lined up opposite of Cheetah and started in on him again.

"Your mama's gotta be real proud. You gotta mama, don't ya? Big fat mama that spends all day cookin' up grits and—"

Cheetah's face became suddenly flushed with anger, and he got out of his stance and stood up. When he did, it drew Highland Park offsides, the end shooting out of his position and knocking Cheetah to the ground. The referees all threw their flags into the air. Cheetah bounced up, his fists clenched at his sides, ready to have it out, then and there.

"Illegal motion, McKinney," said the official as he pointed to Cheetah. "Number 87. Five-yard penalty."

Byron ran up and patted Cheetah on the back. "It's okay. Shake it off."

"Don't let him get to ya," said Gill.

Pete watched from the sidelines, fearful of an altercation, but none came. Cheetah walked to the line, his fists still clenched as he got down in his stance, but he was determined to channel his anger through his shoulder pads instead of his fists.

"Mama's boy, huh?" gloated the Highland Park end. Cheetah didn't say a word. He just dug in his cleats, and when the ball was snapped, he threw a block so hard you could hear the crack of his shoulder pads all the way in the stands. The wind was knocked out of the boy, and he had to be helped off the field.

By the start of the fourth quarter the scoreboard read: McKINNEY LIONS 0—VISITORS 0.

Throughout the final quarter, Highland Park tried to run the halfback around the right end, but each time the defense succeeded in breaking up the play. Gill turned to Cheetah and said, "Watch the halfback comin' around." Cheetah nodded. When the ball was snapped, Cheetah darted past the end and lunged at the halfback's legs, tripping him up for a three-yard loss.

The Highland Park coach signaled for a time-out. The referee blew his whistle, and both teams took off their helmets. A steady drizzle was coming down now, and the people in the stands brought out their umbrellas. But nobody left.

Hoot ran to midfield with a case of Coke bottles filled with water. "Way to go, Lions! Way to hustle!" He patted them all on their shoulder pads and rubbed their helmets. "Doin' a great job on that end, Cheetah. Good work, Gill. Two more minutes. We got 'em beat on penetrations, just dig in and hold 'em, defense; two more minutes!"

The referee signaled for the boys to resume play, and Hoot ran to the sidelines. Highland Park circled together in a huddle while McKinney lined up, digging their cleats into the ground. The Dallas team broke huddle and lined up deep in their own territory on the twenty-yard line. Eighty yards away from the end zone and less than two minutes to get there. No, nobody was leaving the stands, no matter how hard it rained.

On the snap the lines rammed against each other like bighorn sheep butting heads. The Highland Park quarterback nimbly dropped back to pass. His short receivers were covered. He looked up to see the split end sprinting downfield—and launched the long bomb. The Highland Park fans held their breath.

Only one McKinney player had a shot at him. Jeffers. He sprinted across the field, only to see the end make the reception on the fifty. The end stumbled but managed to keep his balance, tightroping down the sidelines to stay in bounds.

Beth, Lynell, and Sue all yelled their lungs out: "GET HIM, BYRON! GET HIM! DON'T LET HIM SCORE!"

Byron dived at the ball carrier, wrapping his arms around the boy's ankles. They both splashed through a puddle and slid to a muddy stop on the thirty-yard line. But the ball didn't go out of bounds so the clock kept on ticking. Byron looked at the scoreboard clock: 1:02 . . . 1:01 . . . 1:00 . . . 0:59 . . . 0:58. He ran to take his defensive position.

The Scotties broke huddle, and the Lions broke theirs, both teams taking their positions in the trenches and digging in. The center hiked the ball, and the quarterback pitched out to the halfback going around the right end—the same play they had run all night long. Cheetah broke through the line and took out one of the blockers, and Byron raced to tackle the ball carrier a few yards past the line of scrimmage.

The clock continued to tick off the seconds: 0:34 . . . 0:33 . . . 0:32.

The Highland Park quarterback waved his arms to get the referee's attention and called time-out.

Byron called his team together, and they all huddled around him as the rain pelted their helmets. "Remember, we got the heart, we got the edge!"

"Come on, let's go!" said Gill.

"We can do it!" said Freight Train.

"It's for Billy; gotta hang tough for Billy!" urged Cheetah.

Highland Park's quarterback came back from the side-lines after conferring with his coach. He huddled up the team, and they spent a long time discussing their next play. Finally, they all clapped and broke huddle.

The McKinney line was already entrenched in the mud, the rain splattering beneath them. Their jaws were clenched; their eyes, set and intense. A smear of blood stretched the length of Gill's shin, and some was smudged across Cheetah's jersey. The time that it took for Highland Park to line up and get set seemed like an eternity.

The quarterback crouched and put his hands under the center. He looked over the line and took note of the placement of the linebackers and defensive backs.

"Hut one! Hut two!"

The play unfolded like a water ballet, the quarterback pivoting, then in one fluid motion pitching out to the halfback—the same play they had just run. McKinney read the play immediately. Cheetah struggled to get past the Highland Park end, but the end fought him every step of the way and finally knocked him off his feet, sending him sliding into the muddy turf.

Gill broke through the line but was slammed to the ground by a pulling guard.

Byron ran with all his strength to meet the runner, but before the halfback crossed the line of scrimmage, he stopped short and pulled back a step, looking for a receiver. The other two backs then formed a wall in front of him and fought off any would-be tacklers. Byron looked over his shoulder to see the left end cutting diagonally across the open field. He wheeled around and went sloshing desperately after him.

Gill pushed himself up and sprinted to reach the halfback from the blind side. Cheetah, his face contorted with an almost primordial sense of determination, scrambled on his hands and knees to reach him. But before either of them could, he lofted the ball over the defense.

Every eye in the stadium was on that ball. The old-age pensioners and Cheetah's and his mother squinted as they tracked it. Gill's family, right down to the youngest, watched the ball as it flew past them. The Highland Park end followed its trajectory through the falling rain but lost the ball in the blur of overhead lights. As the football started its descent, he located it again. He followed the ball's path as it arced downward, adjusting his pace. He followed it downward, downward, until at last it fell into the waiting embrace of his outstretched arms. A few strides after making the catch, he splashed into the end zone, untouched.

The Highland Park squad ran downfield for the point-after attempt, jumping in the air as they ran, celebrating and hugging each other along the way. The kick for the extra point was good. Time ran out for the Lions. When the final gun sounded, the scoreboard read: MCKINNEY LIONS 0— VISITORS 7.

A pall fell over the McKinney side. The fans were devastated. Tears streamed from Beth's face, and Elaine turned to bury her head in Ted's chest. Willard Kincaid closed his eyes. But the feelings in the stands weren't as raw as the ones on the field. Some of the McKinney players dropped to their knees in shock; others fell on their faces, reduced to ruins by the defeat.

Gill stood among the rubble, his helmet dangling from his hand. His face was blank as several of the Highland Park players came to shake his hand. They congratulated him with accolades of respect, like "good game" or "way to play, Thompson," but he didn't even realize they were speaking to him.

Byron was on his knees, his face buried in his hands, blocking out the lights, the crowd, the rain, pushing it all back, never wanting to come out of the darkness that lived behind those hands, never thinking he could look at another McKinney face again.

Cheetah stood dazed as the Dallas fans poured onto the field, streaming around him, celebrating, cheering, searching out Highland Park players to hug. He looked up and saw Byron, a mass of gold and blue clumped on the soggy brown field. He walked through the rain-soaked crowd to reach him, interrupted by the crush of Dallas fans. When at last he reached him, Cheetah touched his shoulder. Byron looked up. Cheetah extended his hand. Byron reached up and grasped it, using it to pull himself up.

Up in the stands Beth was making her way down the bleachers. She pushed through the knots of people that had crowded the aisles and squeezed through a narrow opening in a locked gate that led onto the field. She stood on her tiptoes, searching for Pete, but she couldn't find him anywhere. Then through a broken seam in the crowd she caught a glimpse of him. More desperate now, she called to him, "Pete! Pete!" But the noise of the crowd muted her words.

Pete tried to herd the boys in the direction of the bus, but they wouldn't budge. Forty-eight minutes of playing their hearts out, and it wasn't enough; giving until there was no more to give, and still it wasn't enough.

The McKinney band assembled near the bus. As the boys straggled in from the field, the band played the alma mater.

Pete stood near the door of the bus, trying to get the boys in out of the rain, consoling them and congratulating them for a game so heroically played.

Beth finally made it to the bus and stood next to Pete, putting her arm around him and hugging him. He was fighting to be strong, to be a pillar of support for the team that lay crumbled all around him, but Beth knew from looking into his eyes that he too was beginning to crumble. She entwined her hand in his, as if to infuse him with strength, and she turned to face the boys who were starting to file onto the bus. Byron. Gill. Freight Train. Hoot. Beth could find no words to offer them; only a touch on the arm, a squeeze of the hand, a hug.

The last to get on the bus was Cheetah.

When his eyes met Pete's, he tried to fight back the tears. But it was no use. He fell into Pete's arms, and the two of them locked in a desperate embrace. When he opened his eyes, all he could see was a single stadium pole and the drops of rain that for a moment held the light.

Epilogue

The years proceeded to step themselves off in yard lines of college and career, of children and grandchildren. And before time was finally found to put all of their scattered pictures into scrapbooks, life was about over and done with for Pete and Beth.

Pete was asleep on a couch in the den, the sound of halftime ceremonies spilling into the hallway. His grandson stopped at the doorway and looked at him lying there, then looked to the window that framed his grandmother hanging out the wash.

He tiptoed down the hall, the old attic tugging at his imagination. He creaked up the stairs, his steps growing more timid the closer he got to the top. He reached for the tarnished brass knob and inched open the door. The hinges gave a rusty yawn. He took a tentative step over the threshold. As he did, a scurry of dust took flight through the sun slanting in through the dormer windows. The room smelled of mildew. Against the wall stood an old twin bed, a squadron of school pennants tacked behind it. In the corner stood a halltree draped with a leather jacket. It hung there, a torso of gold with a blue M embossing its chest. The sleeves fell flat and limp, like the withered arms of some long-retired athlete. He stroked the leather sleeves and traced the blue M with his wondering fingers.

To the side of the hall tree stood an old bookshelf, paned

with glass. Against the back of the top shelf was an unframed picture, the weight of forty years slumping it concave and tinting its black and white, sepia. Three rows of football players posed lean and serious-looking; their black high-top shoes, stubbled with cleats; their thinly padded uniforms, shrunk too small. A young, T-shirted coach dared the only smile. Next to him stood a man in work clothes. Two managers crowded together at the other end; the one on one knee, a dwarf.

On top of the bookshelf sat a game ball, gaunt and ruddy and splotched with signatures. He pushed his face toward the glass to read them: COACH PETE WILLIAMS. TED MURPHY. JOHN HENRY "CHEETAH" BROWN. BYRON JEFFERS. GILL THOMPSON. AL "FREIGHT TRAIN" JONES. RAY "HOOT" MAXWELL. BILLY BUTTON.

In front of the team picture rested a wooden paddle. To the one side stood a yearbook. The words *McKinney High* made a diagonal across its padded blue cover; the year, *1946*.

He opened the glass door and pulled the yearbook from the shelf. He sat on the bed and started leafing through its pages.

Sometime later the phone downstairs rang. It rang three times before Pete stumbled into the hall and said, "I got it, Beth." He picked up the receiver. "Hello."

"Hello, Coach," said the voice from the past. "It's the ol' linthead, Cheetah Brown."

"John Henry, is that you?"

"Sure 'nuff."

"Great hearin' your voice. How in the world are ya?"

"Doin' okay, Coach. How 'bout you?"

"Tryin' to adjust to retirement."

"How's Beth?"

"Fine. Babysittin' the grandkids today."

"Listen, reason I called was, I got talkin' with Byron the

other day, and we was tellin' stories, lyin' to each other, and laughin' till we both 'bout got nosebleeds, and well, before we got off the phone, we'd planned a reunion to get the old squad back together again."

"Ya don't say, really?"

"Gonna be a big spread. Everybody's real excited about it. We were thinkin' about the first Saturday in August."

"That would be good for us. Gosh, it'll be great seein' the boys all together again. Lotta good memories, those years in McKinney."

"And some not so good. Like Highland Park. Hard to believe, after all these years, but I still have dreams about that game—dreamin' we're in the last two minutes and still have a chance to win it." He paused a second and then remarked, "Ya know, for a moment there, we were almost heroes."

"For a moment, we were," Pete said. "For a moment, we really were."

There was a long pause, and finally Cheetah said: "I don't mean to rush off, but I'm late pickin' up John, Jr., from practice. He's startin' this year, did I tell ya?"

"I can't believe he's that old."

"Yep. Bigger than I am."

"They grow up fast, don't they?"

"Too fast. Well, tell Beth hello, and we'll be gettin' somethin' in the mail to ya about the reunion."

"Great talkin' with you, John Henry. Love ya."

"I love you too, Coach."

After Pete hung up the phone, he noticed a wedge of light coming from the attic door. He walked up the stairs, which seemed to groan in sympathy with his arthritic knees. He started to close the door when he noticed his grandson asleep on the bed. An old leather helmet sat crookedly on his head. A smattering of yellowed newspaper clippings surrounded him. A football nestled under one arm; a yearbook under the other.

Pete picked up the yearbook and touched the raised letters on its cover.

There was not a championship for Pete during his three years in that town. There would be one waiting for him in another town, at another school. But there would never be another McKinney High. And there would never be another year like 1946.

Sadly, he didn't know it at the time. None of them knew it at the time.